14.95

POW

Tim Reinholt

A big thanks to Monika, Cora and Etta
for your support.
To Ben Ready for your guidance.
To Rex Carrillo for your amazing cover
art.
And to Sam Adams for your
encouragement.

I'm also grateful to all the characters
I've met along the way.

This story takes place in the 1990's, the last decade before computers took over our lives...

1.

POW! The white Ford Mustang punched between two other cars and accelerated away from the accident, the front bumper dragged under the car and then peeled off as the Mustang ran it over. The suspect entered the highway just as three police cars pulled into pursuit behind it. Two brightly colored news helicopters followed the chase from above.

"I say he T-bones a family of nuns in an intersection," said Cliffy as he watched the chase unfold on the 19" TV.

"No way, I bet they get him with a spike strip," Johnny argued. Cliffy, Joneser and Johnny sat on the plush green velvet of 'Oscar the Couch'. Sid sat in the brown rocking recliner chair with a gimballed cup holder screwed to the side of one armrest. As he gently rocked back and forth the can of Olympia nestled in the holder stayed perfectly level.

"Dude, they need to just put him into the wall and end this crap," Joneser snarled, becoming impatient from the lack of carnage. With curly black hair hanging past his shoulders, Matt 'Joneser' Jones had a constant, semi-psychotic glint in his eye that made him look like a young Alice Cooper. He was tall, lanky and claimed to have some Native American heritage. If this were true, it would explain the lack of any facial hair, and his slightly darker complexion.

The other three were generic mid-twenty's white boys. Johnny had dark brown hair that trickled into scruffy beard. His elbows rested on the knees of his faded brown Carhartt pants as he watched the show. A blue plaid flannel hung open exposing a T-shirt he'd gotten free at a beer fest.

Sid's hair was a blond mop of curls barely contained by a faded North Face visor. He wore drab army surplus pants and a tie-dye shirt worn so thin that small holes had formed on the shoulders. A persistant blond soul patch clung to his bottom lip.

Sid, Johnny and Joneser followed the standard look for low budget ski bums. Their clothes were quality brand names, but everything was severely worn and rarely washed.

Cliffy avoided the clichéd ski bum style and kept the look he had maintained in college. His light blond hair was always neatly trimmed and his face clean-shaven. His wardrobe was also a step above the others' and included khaki pants and some nice polo shirts. The innocent straight-edge look was a perfect disguise to help hide his clever and devious nature.

"Nuns don't live in families, man," Sid said as he started to chuckle.

"What?" asked Joneser, confused.

Sid continued, "Cliffy said a 'family of nuns', a group of nuns is like…a…coven or something."

Joneser laughed, "No man, that's witches!"

Cliffy held his index finger up as if delivering an important point and stated, "I believe the correct term is a *'Murder'*, as in, 'I was once attacked by a *Murder* of nuns"

They all laughed and took a sip of cheap beer. Then Johnny pointed excitedly at the TV and exclaimed, "Oh, I called it!" On the screen a police officer was preparing to set the spike strip in front of the speeding car, but the driver veered right at the officer causing him to drop the gear and dive over the barrier. The car avoided the trap and continued on. The sound was off on the TV, and a six-disc CD changer cycled through a variety of classic rock, reggae, gangster rap and techno reflecting the combination of four merged CD collections.

The boys on the couch had their feet kicked up on a low wooden coffee table. A large mushroom design had been carved into the top. Joneser leaned forward and opened a black plastic film canister with a grey top. He poured out a small pile of weed and started picking stems and seeds from the bud and dropping them into an empty beer can. If he found a particularly nice looking seed, he flicked it randomly into the apartment.

Many seeds had fallen to the filthy carpet, and in the back, where the sliding glass door opened to the deck, some seeds even sprouted. Watered by the leaking door and spilled beer, and combined with bright southern aspect sunlight, the brave little weed plants would sprout, grow about an inch, then topple over and die.

Joneser reached for a Evian water bottle that had been fitted with a metal bowl a few inches below the neck. Aquarium air hose ran from the bowl's stem into a few inches of brown, smelly bong water at the bottom of the bottle. He packed the homemade bong with weed and pulled a strong lungful of smoke in. He exhaled with a few snorts then said, "the best chase was that dude who stole the city bus. He was just plowing through everything!"

Sid grinned as he recalled the image of destruction and agreed. "That was sweet."

The fact that they had cable TV at all was courtesy of a late night engineering project. The boys' apartment was on the second floor of the Whispering Pines apartment complex. In the apartment above them lived two snowboarders from California, it was assumed they were trust funders. The boarders were rarely seen and never interacted with any other tenants in the building.

Late one night, Sid and Joneser had opened the cable outlet cover attached to the wall. Nothing was connected to the outlet for their apartment, but the active coaxial cable was visible running through the wall to the other apartment. They carefully pulled the slack cable through the hole and installed a three-way splice from Radio Shack into the wire. When that was done, they connected it to their own outlet and reinstalled the cover. So far they were going on eight months with free cable, as long as the upstairs neighbors continued to pay the bill.

"The problem is, people always try to escape in cars on roads," Johnny stated.

"Yeah you never see a jet ski escaping down the road!" Sid added with a giggle.

"No not a jet ski in the road, ass, but...like a jet ski up a river."

"Oh yeah!" Joneser sat up as an idea came to his stony mind, "or mountain bikes! My friend down at CU said the Boulder cops are cruising around on bikes. How sick would it be to have a high-speed urban mountain bike chase? Man I'm tellin' you, I would drop any flabby cop who tried to catch me. You could lead them down flights of stairs and off drops!"

"Those bike cops suck," Cliffy said flatly, "I was selling acid on The Hill one time to a couple of freshman and two of those cops just rolled up quietly right next to us."

"No shit?" Sid looked at him perplexed. "How are you not in prison?"

"Well," Cliffy smiled, "the freshmen *thought* it was acid, but even the cops could see that it was just a few small squares I had cut off of a playing card." This brought a round of groans from the group.

Johnny smiled, "Cliffy, you bring dishonor to the sterling reputation of all drug dealers."

"Yeah isn't there some code of ethics, or something?" Joneser asked, "You should be kicked out of the union... or disbarred."

Cliffy defended himself, "Hey, it's not my fault those kids were born with no brains and tons of money. In fact I'd say it was my obligation to exploit such a weakness."

"Cheers to that," said Sid as he finished his can of Olympia and got up to get another.

Johnny managed to find his original train of thought and continued. "It's like, every car chase is just playing into the cop's hands, you know? They have radios and they can set up other units ahead of you, they know where the choke points are. And when a helicopter catches up to you, you're done".

"All valid points" Sid confirmed as he returned to the seat, handed out beers and then pulled the tab on a fresh can.

Joneser said to Johnny, "Fortunately for the world we keep your criminal mastermind safely contained in this apartment, and stoned." He offered the loaded Evian bong to Johnny.

Johnny waved the bong away and replied, "No way, that thing tastes like melted plastic." He pulled a small wooden box from his pocket, slid open the top and a ceramic one-hitter pipe colored to look like a cigarette sprang out of the spring-loaded holder.

The others groaned and called him a "bong snob."

Sid looked aghast. "How dare you say that my ghetto trash pipe tastes like melted plastic?"

"I'm just saying we need to get another bong...Cliff." He turned to glare at Cliff.

Two weeks earlier Cliffy had the idea of filling the apartment's old bong with the season's first snow and smoking on the balcony. Unfortunately he left it outside, the snow melted, and then refroze, cracking the bottom of the bong. No one was particularly mad at Cliff. Just no one had any extra money to purchase a new one.

Johnny tried in defeat to blow through his one-hitter, but found it to be thoroughly plugged with resin, the tar-like substance left over when pot is burned. He opened the one large drawer in the coffee table and sorted through the lighters and rolling papers until he found the appropriate poking device: a single bicycle spoke. It had been cut down to about eight inches with the rounded nipple end serving as a handle. The other end was already coated with sticky resin. He started a cycle of heating the pipe with a lighter then pushing at the resin buildup with the poker, hoping to clear the bore.

It was nearly eleven o'clock on a Tuesday night, during the magical time of year in the Colorado ski town of Crested Butte known as 'preseason'. The first snowstorm had already teased the locals into believing this would be a big year even though it was only the end of October. A new crop of hopeful skiers and snowboarders were steadily flowing into town, fighting for decent living spaces and decent jobs, both of which were limited. The boys were going on their third year in CB. This made them hardened locals. The exception was Cliffy, who had visited many times while he finished college in Boulder, but he had moved up permanently the previous spring. This explained why his *room* was a corner of the hallway partitioned off with a hanging blanket. Sid and Jonny shared the one bedroom while Joneser lived in a small cage-like loft hanging from the ceiling.

Overcrowding, and filling apartments and houses beyond normal capacity was commonplace in all ski towns. The combination of high rent and low paying jobs required it. This often led to miserable living conditions with roommate drama, but the boys were successful because their similar personalities meshed perfectly together. No one strived for social dominance. If someone had a good story, or something to say, the others genuinely listened. In their own ways each of them contributed to the function of the apartment. And if any of them had a bad idea and needed encouragement, the others quickly added fuel to the fire.

The CD player randomly cycled on to the Peter Tosh hit 'Legalize it' and began to play. The boys grooved on the mellow beat and familiar scratch guitar. Sid spoke up, interrupting the chorus. "This song starts out strong, but then it kinda falls apart at the end."

"What do ya' mean?" asked Joneser.

"The goats and the ants," answered Cliff knowingly.

"Yeah, exactly," continued Sid nodding at Cliff. "It's like Tosh set out to create the anthem that would lead the revolution to legalize ganja. This song was going to be the rallying cry for millions, so he comes up with all these valid reasons to legalize."

The others shifted their gaze to Sid as they recognized a great stoner monologue forming before them. Johnny kept poking into his pipe, pulling out the spoke and wiping sticky resin on a paper towel.

Sid went on, "First he explains that everyone in these important jobs, doctors, lawyers and judges all smoke it. Then he lists medical conditions that can be treated with THC like flu and asthma, and whatever the fuck 'Thrombosis' is. So far so good, then just like that, he goes off the rails, and is like..." Sid adopted a bad Jamaican accent, 'I dunno mon, I can't tink of anytin else.' "So he comes up with 'ants eat it and goats like to lay in it?' Sid stopped for a moment and the song finished a chorus then went on to the verse he had just described.

Johnny listened to the line and agreed, "Yeah, that's kinda dumb."

Cliffy thought for a moment then said, "Maybe he smoked a spliff after he finished each verse, and by the time he got to that one he was just blazed out of his gourd." Sid relaxed and sat back in the chair, feeling a sense of accomplishment for presenting his observation to the others.

Johnny felt he was making progress. Three quarters of the pipe were clean with one stubborn blob of goo sealing the narrow end of his one-hitter. His buzz had worn off and he was starting to crave one more puff before calling it a day. "Do you guys know how Peter Tosh died?" Johnny asked, indicating he had a story to add to the topic.

Joneser answered, "He was shot."

Johnny nodded and continued "Yeah, but here's the thing. At the time he was like, an international reggae super star with gold records and world tours, and he got shot in a Kingston ghetto over a drug deal gone bad!"

Joneser shook his head incredulously and started to say "Dude, that's not what..."

"Seriously!" Johnny cut him off, "I'm telling you; drugs always get you in the end." Johnny arranged himself for one final push. He cupped the pipe in one open palm while he pushed the sharpened spoke as hard as he could into the pipe with his other hand. Suddenly, the resin plug let go and Johnny let out a gasp as he instantly pushed the spoke through the pipe, through his palm and out the backside of his left hand. He let go of the spoke and held both hands out in front of him like a wide-eyed magician revealing the Amazing Balancing Cigarette trick!

The others reacted in horror and awe as if high voltage had just run through them, sitting bolt upright and yelling. Johnny snapped out of his shock, grabbed the spoke and yanked it back out of his hand. This garnered another round of pained and disgusted cries from the other three.

"DUDE! We could have cut the end off and just pulled it though!" exclaimed Sid with a baffled look on his face. Cliffy jumped into action and ran for the first aid kit in the bathroom. The apartment may frequently run out of toilet paper and laundry soap, but the first aid kit was a sacred necessity always kept replenished. Cliff helped Johnny clean the wound with iodine and applied a bandage as Sid wiped up drops of blood from the floor. Joneser held up the one hitter with the bloody spoke still sticking through it and stared at it in awe. He wiped the resin and blood off the spoke with the paper towel, pulled the pipe off the spoke and wiped the end. Then he stuck it in his mouth and blew through it. Finally, with an approving nod, he said, "This is really clean now".

2.

The next morning the rising sun hit the highest peaks first and bathed them in a golden light known as alpenglow. Then the sunlight appeared to follow gravity and flowed down each mountain and into the box canyon that hid the small town of Crested Butte. 13,000 foot mountains stood to the west and north of town with the jagged fortress looking butte to the east giving the town its namesake. Thirty miles south through the canyon lay the town of Gunnison with the closest fast food or proper grocery store. CB was an isolated community that no tourists visited by accident. No one passed by here on their way to someplace else. If you ended up in town there had to be a reason. Many pilgrims were skiers and snowboarders. Drawn like junkies to a fix or a congregation to church, once you became addicted to the almighty force of Gravity, little else mattered in life.

For young men it was very much like joining a monkhood. You dedicated yourself to a life of poverty, with little material possessions except for your ski gear. You committed yourself to a life of near celibacy. The typical ski town ratio was ten guys to every one girl. And this force that you committed to often called for blood sacrifices. No one escaped the ski bum life unharmed. Knee's, wrists, legs, arms and backs all fell beneath the wrath of Gravity. It was this element of commitment that weeded out the weak and made the survivors into a tight band.

Sid rose from bed and scrounged through the kitchen putting together a quick breakfast. Since his job as a snowcat operator hadn't officially started yet, he was assisting the ski area vehicle mechanics while they finished the summer maintenance. Joneser smelled the frying eggs, climbed down from his loft in boxer shorts and stumbled to the kitchen bleary eyed. He too had to get to the ski area and perform his job with the chair lift mechanics preparing the lifts for a long, trouble-free winter. "How's Johnny's hand?" he asked Sid.

"Eh, it stopped bleeding pretty quickly, and he took some Vitamin I."

"I'm sure that resin cover spoke was pretty clean, he did sterilize it with his lighter before skewering himself," Joneser grinned.

"Fuuuuck yoooou," Johnny yawned as he walked in holding up his bandaged left hand with his middle finger extended. He reached into the cupboard, pulled out a box of knock-off Lucky Charms called Lucky Stars and poured himself a bowl.

Cliffy soon woke up and joined them. He and Johnny didn't need to be at work until later in the day, but they wanted to join the morning wake and bake ritual. Johnny relented and took a big hit from the home-made bong, despite receiving grief from the others.

Sid and Joneser, packed lunches, and headed out the door. Four stairs up from the bottom of the staircase Sid jumped out and landed squarely on the last wooden step with both feet. The spongy rotten wood flexed, but didn't give. Joneser pulled the same move but jumped even higher and harder. His feet pounded into the last step and it gave a loud CRACK. While this seemed like a senseless act of vandalism, the boys, as well as the other tenants of the building viewed it as a public safety service. The staircase all the way to the third flood was rotten and dangerously unstable. Some sections of railing were visibly pulling the nails out of the wall.

Yet, despite numerous complaints over several years the landlord refused to make such an expensive repair. So, all the tenants made an effort to slowly make the staircase worse until repairs could not be avoided. Many tenants aggressively wiggled the railings as they made their way up and down the stairs. The boys focused their energy on the last step, and hoped to gradually break steps from the bottom leading up.

There was no love lost between the occupants of apartment 203 and the owner of Whispering Pines. When Sid and Johnny had been shown the apartment by the landlord it had contained a full size stove and refrigerator. They paid first, last and a deposit and were told they could move in after the apartment was "cleaned and prepped," over the weekend. When they unlocked the door on Monday they found the fridge and stove had been replaced with used half-size appliances. The counters just ended with an eight-inch gap on either side of the stove. And the small fridge stood in the unpainted outline of its larger predecessor. The owner deflected their complaints, stating it was all perfectly legal, hidden within the fine print of the lease.

It was Sid's idea to sabotage the fridge, the stove was manageable, but the tiny fridge soon became a solid cube of ice in the freezer section and nearly room temperature in the fridge section. The owner advised them to defrost it once a week. Sid pulled the fridge away from the wall, opened the rear panel and one at a time started unplugging connections. When he unplugged one that made the motor turn off, he carefully pulled the wire terminal out of the plastic connector. Pried the crimp off of the copper wire, cut off the strands of copper and crimped the terminal solidly on to the plastic insulation of the wire. When it was assembled it looked like a solid connection, but no electricity ran through it. Plus, it would take a somewhat skilled electrician to find the flaw.

Luckily, the building handyman was not a skilled electrician; the owner watched as the handy man scratched his head and declared, "Yep, she's dead". The owner begrudgingly installed a new full size fridge, and, the trust between both parties was gone forever. Shortly after, Joneser moved into the loft and eventually Cliffy moved into the crowded apartment. This was the arrangement in many of the units. People slept on couches, bunk beds, in closets or simply hung curtains in hallways to create more spaces.

The overall atmosphere of the Whispering Pines apartment building was that of a pirate ship, rowdy, overcrowded and smelling of funk. By an unfortunate design the main sign on the front of the building was assembled with large wooden letters that could easily be removed and swapped. Such as it was, that the "E" and the "I" in "Pines" spent roughly half of the time spelling "The Whispering Penis."

3.

Sid and Joneser made the short commute to the mountain in Sid's monstrous forest green 1973 Ford Galaxy 500. The four door sedan eased into the dirt parking lot already half filled with old and new pickup trucks, battered compact cars and one other 70's luxury barge. A spot was open next to Don the carpenter's 1975 Dodge Monaco and Sid parked his Ford next to its peer. He always felt that the two cars shared stories while they spent the day next to each other, reminiscing about the good 'ol days.

The large building was the only one in sight out in this far corner of ski area property. It housed the three departments of Building, Chair Lift and Vehicle maintenance. On all sides it was surrounded by various pieces of machinery and specialty equipment. Rows of snowmobiles or "sleds" were arranged for the ski patrollers, lift mechanics, snow makers and others. Next to the sleds were parked the mountain's fleet of snowcats the majority of these were identical with a blade on the front and a tiller mounted to the rear that groomed the snow into perfect corduroy as it went along. Scattered among the fleet were some of the specialty cats including three winch cats. Two were set up for grooming the steep runs and the third had a tall crescent shaped Pipe Dragon mounted to the front. This was the cat that carved the perfect transitions of the halfpipe.

Final repairs and summer maintenance were being done on several of the cats. Close to the shop one cat sat on its rubber bogey wheels with its tracks removed, this was where Sid's task came in. He and Jonah, another cat driver, had the miserable job of tightening all the bolts that held the aluminum teeth, or "growsers' to the rubber belts making up the track. When they noticed a cracked or broken growser, they had to remove it and replace it with a new one. The tracks were positioned on their edges and formed into a big 'S' pattern to allow then to stand up like a big piece of ribbon. Aside from the basic monotony of a job like this, it also required one person to be running a air impact wrench on one side of track, while the other person held a straight two-foot breaker bar and socket on the other side.

Neither job was pleasant, the air gun was heavy and loud, and the bar rattled and pounded who ever held on to it. Strangely enough, Sid and Jonah were incredibly grateful to be offered this brutal

16

position. All the other cat drivers were simply laid off for the summer, some left town, while others got seasonal jobs. These two had been offered the positions of "mechanic's helpers," for the summer because they both had basic mechanical aptitude, and showed up to work on time. Earlier in the summer the guys had been performing oil changes and greasing the machines, but the last three weeks were solid track work.

Sid stopped in the break room for a cup of the terrible shop coffee, made small talk with the various electricians, carpenters and mechanics from other departments, then, with arms still aching from the day before he and Jonah picked up their tools and headed out to the track. The rattling air gun didn't allow for any conversation, so Jonah plugged a battered boom box tape player into an extension cord. Then he rifled through a shoebox full of cassettes and pulled out what he knew to be Metallica's Master of Puppets. The white print on the smoke colored cassette was almost completely worn off, and he could see through the side that the spool of tape had loosened into a wide coil. He pulled a yellow pencil from the box, threaded it into the cogged wheel of the cassette and wound the tape by hand until all the slack was taken up. Then he popped the cassette into the player and pushed play. Searing guitar chords burst from the tinny speakers as the air gun began to rattle the first bolt of the day.

Joneser listened to a short briefing among the lift mechanics and the lift operations manager, then he and another junior mechanic, Dave, were teamed up with two of the senior techs Scorch and Thumper. Nicknames among the Lift Ops crew were colorful and hard earned. Each one had a story behind it dating back years, and the history of each name wasn't given out easily to every new guy who came along. Only once you were truly accepted as a bona fide member of the team, would you begin to hear the origin stories of each cryptic moniker.

Most positions at the ski area worked on an unofficial apprenticeship program. Turnover among the senior employees was very low, so even though Joneser had been with this crew for two and a half years he still took his place next to Dave in the bed of the rugged blue 1980 Chevy 4x4 pickup as Thumper sat in the shotgun seat and Scorch got behind the wheel. Without snow, the ski area is crisscrossed with miles of dirt access roads. These roads received no maintenance, so they were rutted and wash boarded to a brutal degree. Each morning the ride up the mountain was slow and almost pleasant. But at the end of a long day, when cold beer was calling the men down from the mountain, riding in the bed of the truck became a terrifying experience.

The truck eased its way into a position under the Paradise Express lift line. The crew all donned safety harnesses and split into pairs. Joneser and Thumper climbed the access ladder up tower ten while the others headed for tower nine. High above the ground, the two men reached the small work platform and secured safety lines. They then began a meticulous inspection of all the components that made up the top of the chair lift tower. Joneser checked each of the sheave wheels that the cable rides on. He measured the wear and tested the bearings. While Thumper used an electronic meter to verify the safety switch would function correctly and stop the lift if the cable were to come off track. They also looked over all the welds and joints of the cross arm assembly looking for any wear or damage. If there were any defcts in the metal structure, they would return with a truck-mounted welder, grind out the crack and fill it back in with fresh metal.

Welding repairs were truly Thumper's expertise; he was an artist with liquid metal. The crew joked that he could weld tinfoil to an I beam he was so skilled. Joneser respected him highly and always paid attention to any advice he offered.

Thumper also played another key role on the team. He and Wally the master electrician, never smoked weed, but curiously every time random drug tests were ordered on the department- it was these two who had to go take the whiz quiz. The rest of the crew was thankful to these two and also someone in high-level management who had arranged such a sustainable program. The owners of the ski area knew they couldn't afford to lose most of their employees to drug testing.

Joneser firmly held the rail and leaned out to the farthest sheave on the sheave train, with almost nothing beneath him he was looking forty feet down to the ground.

" Hang on tight" said Thumper, " I know a guy in Oregon who jumped from this high and broke both legs."

Joneser turned to him with one eyebrow arched, "Why would anyone jump from a tower?"

18

"Well you would too if you saw what was coming at him. You see, they had all the chairs off and had just strung a new cable top to bottom, now they needed to make the splice. So they had flown in a team of splice specialists from France, like, that's what these guys did for a living. They were putting the two ends together in the lower terminal building and they had the massive counter weight held up with a big wheel loader. My friend is up on top of the first tower working to make sure the cable stayed put on both sets of sheaves.

Anyway, the splicer says he needs a little tension, so lower the weight just a little bit, the kid in the loader pushes the wrong lever and dumps the counter weight instead. Well, the splice wasn't finished! So it let loose and snapped like a two inch steel rubber band, it whips through the terminal and starts flying up the mountain. My buddy sees both ends of the cable coming towards him and knows that he's gonna get cut clean in half if they hit him. So he bails off the tower!"

"Duuude," said Joneser as he shook his head and contemplated the story he had just heard. Ski town stories were a backbone of the culture. In a good story the content and delivery mattered far more than the facts. Joneser wondered if Thumper really knew the guy who jumped, probably not, this story had simply been passed on to Thumper from another source separated several degrees from the actual event. Could something like this actually happen? The odds were likely, it all sounded very probable. Maybe it didn't happen exactly the way Thumper told the story, but he certainly didn't make it up out of thin air. Joneser recalled a line he had read regarding stories about the Viet Nam war. It explained that any story that sounds outlandish and unbelievable, is probably a toned down version of an event that was in fact, even more incredible than the story. He tended to feel this way about mountain town stories as well.

Regardless of the facts, Thumpers story had scored its intended points. Joneser glanced at the thick steel cable he held in his hand and processed the immense potential energy contained in it. Then his mind went to the incompetent machine operator who released the weight, whether or not this person existed, Joneser swore to himself he would never be the guy whose mistake caused injury to a coworker. He would never move the lever the wrong way, and he needed to stop smoking pot before work.

Thumper clapped his hands together and declared "I think tower ten will be fine for another season, I'll see if those guys found anything." He thumbed the walkie-talkie held firmly in a harness across his chest, "Scorch, how you guys doing? Find anything?"

The radio crackled a quick response from Scorch "A-OK for the most part, but, looks like water has gotten into the connection for this sensor and it's starting to corrode"

"Nice catch" Thumper responded, "We don't want any green grodies living in our safety switches" referring to the green fungus like corrosion that developed in electrical components once water had intruded. "We're headed to eleven" he notified Scorch as he headed for the ladder.

4.

It was Saturday, the day of Halloween, and the boys were in #203 assembling their costumes with supplies they had gathered mostly from thrift stores and storage closets. Joneser looked imposing with silver painted cardboard forming an armored chest piece over a sleeveless, dirty, brown t-shirt, more cardboard with metal rivets made gauntlets on each fore arm. A broad leather belt turned into a headband held back his long black hair. Thick red face paint stripes ran from each eye down his cheeks.

But the masterpiece hung from another leather belt on his hip, it was a full-size steel broad sword he had spent hours on in the ski area welding shop. Formed of scrap, it was heavy, cumbersome and tried to pull his pants off his waist if his hand didn't support it. When he wielded it menacingly he looked like someone Conan the Barbarian would have killed.

Sid had on tight red sweatpants with black bikini shorts over them. On the table in front of him he had a red long sleeve t-shirt spread out. Next to it were small bottles of silver and black paint and a brush. "I give up man, I have no idea what the Greatest American Hero had for an emblem," he said in frustration.

"Wasn't it like…a trident? Or something" Johnny offered.

"I'm telling you, it was a swastika," said Joneser the Destroyer.

"It was NOT a fucking swastika!" Sid responded with a laugh.

"But it could be." Joneser came back with a mischievous smirk, "You could tell people you are Uber Man"

"People always love a good Nazi themed costume," Cliff chimed in.

"I think I'll just make a big 'G'" said Sid, ignoring his roommates. "And people can figure it out."

Before long, Sid stood in the living room with his face clean-shaven and his blond curls brushed into a curly white-boy afro. He had the red suit on and a long cape of black fabric hanging off his back, making it a decent super hero costume.

Next to the barbarian on the couch sat Cliff in a white polo shirt with fluffy white rabbit ears on his head, a round cotton tail on the back of his pants and a bunny nose stuck to his face with an elastic string. He was rolling short, stubby joints from a big sack of weed and closing them into colored plastic Easter eggs that he was piling in an Easter basket.

It was only a short walk to town, but the boys, like most of the locals in town, rode their cherished 'Townie' bikes. Mountain bikes were a much too costly investment for everyday use, so a second older and simpler bike was needed for moving around town. Over the years hundreds of old clunker bikes from the fifties's and sixties's had migrated into this town. These ranged from rust colored no-name bikes to vintage Schwinns with names like 'Hornet' and 'Corvette'. Cliff rode a faded blue girls bike with no legible identification. Johnny had a red Schwinn classic he called "The 'fifty seven'" due to its build date. Joneser's lanky build wasn't comfortable on the low cruiser bikes; he preferred to sit more upright on a white Sears commuter bike with a milk crate mounted to a rack on the back that currently held a six pack of Coors.

Completing the pack as they rode four wide down the empty street was Sid on a bike he truly loved. He had found the 50's era Firestone Silver Cruiser men's bike at a pawnshop in Denver. It was unique in town because of its fully chromed frame and fenders. Schwinn bikes may have had an air of superiority, but they never made a chromed frame like this.

The streets only had lamps at intersections, and as they pedaled through one long section of darkness, no one noticed two other riders glide silently up behind them, only to scream like banshees in unison as they pulled in close. The boys startled and swerved. Cliffy flinched and slipped a pedal making him veer into Joneser who was carrying his giant sword across his handlebars. His left hand lost its grip and the heavy blade swung down to clang off his front fender. Everyone stopped and turned to see who had so deftly assaulted them. The two riders were laughing hysterically as the boys recognized Wes from the bike shop. He normally had a bushy red beard to go with his shoulder length red hair, but tonight it was shaved into a goatee and Fu Manchu mustache. He wore a green bathrobe with a Mickey Mouse t-shirt underneath.

"HA, HA, HA, assholes," Sid said sarcastically. He was still shaken from the scare, but realized Wes had reproduced the look of Eric Stoltz's character from Pulp Fiction, with one exception. "What? You couldn't find a Speed Racer shirt?"

Wes shrugged "Hey, I tried," by now Joneser had gathered himself and held the broad sword ready at his side. Wes got a full view of the warrior and took a step back, "Holy shit! If I knew you looked like that, we wouldn't have messed with you"

Joneser pointed the sword at Wes' throat and snarled in a pseudo Russian accent "I should cut off your head, you made me dent my fender."

Wes smiled and held up his hands in surrender. Cliffy stepped forward and observed the outfit of the second rider. He was tall with long brown hair pulled into a ponytail and his face painted red. He had a pencil thin mustache and wore a sharp grey business suit with printed $100 bills sticking out of each jacket pocket. The Easter Bunny took a long look and tapped his chin as if in deep thought then said " I feel like I've met you before, did I once sell my soul to you?"

"Not yet, but soon enough you will" replied another friend from the bike shop, Arliss, speaking like a mix of game show host and used car salesman. "I'm the CEO of Snow Corp, nice to meet ya." He grinned as he shook Cliff's hand.

"Nice" said Johnny, "that's a good one."

Snow Corp was a massive corporation that had started buying up ski areas a few years earlier. They had just bought the nearby mountain of Aspen and rumor was they had an eye on CB. For all the locals, Snow Corp represented an Evil Empire that buys up ski areas and real estate, then develops them into playgrounds for the rich and drives out the working class. Arliss' costume was a perfect representation of what most people thought of the company.

Wes padded his pockets like he was looking for something then said, "Hey we were gonna burn one, but I don't have a pipe, Johnny can we use your hand?"

"That is so funny," Johnny deadpanned as the others laughed at him.

Wes said, "I was just kidding... I don't need a pipe." Then he put a large joint to his mouth and lit it. The six of them finished the joint as they rolled up to their friend's house on Whiterock Ave. They parked their bikes among all the other townies in the driveway and headed in to the party.

The small house was full of costumed partiers, and the music could barely be heard over the din of conversation. They greeted Nick and Dani a couple who owned the house next door. Nick wore bright yellow foul weather gear with big waterproof rubber boots. He looked like the fisherman on a box of Gorton's fish sticks. The costume seemed a little random until his fiancé Dani shuffled into the room in a bikini top and her lower half wrapped in shimmering green cloth that looked like scales. Over her feet she had a large green foam rubber flipper. Dani had to hop or shuffle everywhere she moved, but it still wasn't the most cumbersome costume in the house.

Sid noticed some people talking to a huge elaborate costume of Sesame Street's Count. His head was a sphere nearly three feet across with ears sticking out even further. The eyes and face all looked finely crafted from papier-mache and cardboard. Sid got closer and noticed one of the count's hands held a tall drink and a clear rubber hose ran from the drink up into the giant mouth. As the other folks walked away Sid ducked and looked under the triangle fangs deep into the Count's mouth. Far back where the throat would start he recognized the face of one of the locals, Pete 'Racin' Mason. "Dude, this thing is awesome, how'd you even get in here?" he asked.

"Oh it was a bitch," he replied. "My wife always makes my costumes," he explained, "and she knows that if I can, I'll hit every party, so she makes my costume bulkier each year. Did you see my hammer head shark last year?"

"Oh yeah," Sid recalled, "You had fins on your arms with no hand holes."

"Yeah, that didn't last." said Pete, as the conversation turned to the impending winter, and other ski related topics.

After about an hour, Joneser held his sword aloft and loudly declared he was off to pillage the town. The Easter Bunny passed out some eggs, and then hopped behind him, followed by the Greatest American Hero who raised both hands up and attempted to fly towards the door. Failing that, he crashed into the counter knocking over some empty beer cans. Johnny had been talking to a cute girl dressed as a ladybug and decided to stay, but wished the others 'good luck' as they left.

The three riders each pounded one of Joneser's beers as they cruised on to the main drag. Sid was sitting upright and riding with no hands as he tipped his head back to finish the beer. Suddenly he felt a tug at his neck and wildly waved his hands about trying to grab the handlebars and regain his balance. The beer fell to the ground as Sid and his bike collapsed in a shower of sparks on the pavement. His two friends rushed over in disbelief at what they had just seen. When they found him unwinding his cape from the hub of the rear wheel, they burst into laughter so hard they could barely stand up. The pounding in his hip told Sid tonight's shenanigans would leave a bruise, and he grimly limped the rest of the way to the bar pushing his bike as the tire loudly rubbed against the fender.

The bar was packed wall to wall with the standard display of slutty pirate girls, Denver Broncos and vampires. Scattered among them were people without costumes, or costumes that just made little sense like, 'Flannel Man', or the two 'Zombie Care Bears'. Sid commented that there were probably more people dressed as Doctors and hospital staff than actually worked in the town as hospital staff. Joneser's menacing look cleared a path through the crowd and up the stairs to the second floor. Once upstairs, the boys gathered some other friends, lit up one of Cliffy's joints, and started passing it around. After a few puffs Sid felt much better, but noticed he had actually torn a hole in the side of his pants during the crash, and his cape now had a big patch of grease on it from the bike chain.

Sid looked around and spotted Joneser talking to a girl with blue face paint, long blond pigtails and a white beanie. It took a moment to figure out she was Smurfette, and it looked like her and the Barbarian were hitting it off as they talked and laughed. Cliffy had sparked another joint and a new crowd was forming around him. Sid decided to go back down stairs to the bar. As he was waiting for a chance to order a two-dollar PBR, he heard a commotion from the front entrance. He watched dumbfounded as four guys in khaki safari shirts and hats, riding ostriches, came bursting into the bar.

They ran wildly through the crowd, bumping into people and sloshing drinks. Then after less than a minute the riders turned their mounts and disappeared out the door as quickly as they had come. Sid tried to get a good look at the last one as it was exiting, and his brain slowly processed that the costumes were the neck and body of the giant bird attached to the man's waist. The legs hanging off the saddle were fake and the bird's legs were the man's legs with yellow tights and big three toed feet over his shoes. Sid shook his head smiling and mentally registered the bird riders as the best costume he'd seen tonight, possibly ever.

Sid was still two or three people away from actually getting up to the bar. Two bartenders at the other end were furiously slinging drinks as fast as they could. However, the one closest to Sid was casually chatting up a girl with long dreadlocks, and ignoring the throngs of people with money in hand. Typical ski town service, he was thinking to himself when he was violently shoved by the barbarian with the Easter Bunny in tow. "Dude," Joneser declared, "we're going to the A frame."

As they filed out, Sid noticed that Smurfette was following along. Once outside, she introduced herself as Jenny and explained that Joneser had invited her to the next party. Jenny had her own cruiser bike, and as they rode the few blocks to their destination Sid tried to explain the Bird riders to his friends.

He hadn't done a very good job explaining, and as they parked their bikes in the backyard of a large A frame house, the others were questioning whether Sid had hallucinated the whole experience. The A frame had a large fenced yard, and the occupants were kind enough to let Joneser and Sid leave their sleds parked here for the summer.

Before going into the party, Sid wandered to the far corner of the lot and gave the sleds a quick look. The tarps were still bungee corded tight over the hoods and seats. And the sleds were elevated off the ground with a milk crate under the front of each and wood propping the rear suspension off the ground. The paddle tracks hung loose under the small bogey wheels with all the tension released.

Sid leaned in close to his sled and gave it a slight shake. He didn't hear any mice scurrying inside and hoped that meant that none had moved under his hood to wreak havoc on his wires and fuel lines. He had bought the Skidoo new two years ago and only had three more years of payments. The winter he had knee surgery he couldn't ski, so he walked into the dealership and made a deal with the Devil. It was the biggest financial responsibility he had undertaken in his life, and he treated it with loving respect. He religiously cleaned the clutches, greased the suspension and made sure nothing was coming loose or wearing out. His trusty steed sat dormant in its summer hibernation, but soon it would be let loose on the mountains once again.

Sid quietly pissed on the wooden fence in the darkness of the backyard. He glanced up and noticed that the crescent moon that had been shining clearly earlier was now only a glow behind a cloudbank. A light wind kicked up and he thought that it felt very comfortable for the last night of October. It occurred to him that a warm breeze could indicate a massive cold front moving in, flushing all the warm air out in front of it. He grinned as he fixed his sweatpants and headed for the party house as the music of Sublime spilled out into the night.

He came through the back door and found someone in a fox mask and a Hawiian shirt hanging out in the kitchen. The kitchen table held a large bowl of fruit punch and alcohol, as well as some chips and dip. He grabbed a handful of chips, then proceeded through the doorway and found a seat on the carpeted floor of the living room. The walls sloping inward from both sides gave the house a cozy feel. A colorful tapestry was pinned to the ceiling, turning the room into a big cocoon.

A thick cloud of pot smoke filled the room and standing in the center was none other than The Count! Pete finished packing a glass bowl and handed to a person next to him. He explained that the weed was a Cannabis Cup winner named "The Cough." Sid took a big hit and leaned back closing his eyes.

Tranquility settled over the group as some recounted stories of mountain biking or kayaking over the summer. Pete was an avid kayaker, and he owned a local auto repair shop. Often, a blue-sky afternoon and high water on the river were just too precious to ignore. He'd close up shop, then he and the other mechanics would grab their boats. This made for a slim paycheck, but summer in C.B. is too limited of a resource to waste. It was also known around town that if you ever noticed Pete's white VW bug up at the top of the river, where he had put in, he'd be very grateful if you would grab the key from behind the gas fill door, and drive the bug down to where he would take out. Little acts of random kindness like this, and a 'pay it forward,' mentality added to the charm of the little mountain town.

The first floor of the A frame was divided into three equal sections. Arliss rented a room that the front door opened into. The middle was the living room and the kitchen was in the rear, ending at the back door. The upstairs loft belonged to Kevin, his girlfriend Chrissy and their black lab Jory. This seemed like a wonderful way to end the evening, everyone winding down into a chill, mellow atmosphere.

Suddenly, the mood was shattered as people began filling the kitchen area and pouring punch from the bowl. Within minutes the room was full of loud, obnoxious drunks.

The stoners quickly realized that the bars had just shut the doors at two AM. Now the bar crowd was loose on the town like a horde of zombies, seeking more booze and a place to party. Pete took off his enormous Count Head and stood up, Sid also jumped into action. The two of them made for the kitchen area to secure the punch bowl and the rest of the liquor in the fridge. Pete was in his thirties, which made him a figure of authority amongst the drunken twenty-somethings. He grabbed the stack of SOLO cups from the table and pulled the ladle away from a kid who looked sixteen.

Sid felt adrenaline energizing him and knowing Pete had his back gave him an air of confidence. He quickly scanned the crowd of invaders for familiar faces. The few who belonged here, he guided into the other room. He then questioned the strangers if they knew who lived here. When he was met with dumb looks he herded the group back out the door. Two girls who were obviously used to getting their way, refused to leave, stating they had been invited. Sid started back pedaling, losing ground to the pushy bar bitches. Luckily Pete took command and explained to them that the party was over and they should go home. They walked out leaving a flurry of insults and alcohol fumes.

As the crowd dissolved and Sid secured the back door, he learned that earlier someone had yelled out in front of the bar, "Party on Sopris Avenue!" Whoever incited this invasion deserved a hard punch in the nuts. Sid headed to the front of the house when loud shouts of aggression could be heard in the far room. When he opened the door he struggled to fathom the scene he was witnessing. Three guys Sid didn't recognize were arguing with Kevin, the host. They were demanding to be allowed into the party. Sid caught sight of Cliffy and Joneser standing ready to jump in with Kevin if needed. He also noticed Chrissy, Kevin's girlfriend watching intently. Chrissy was dressed in a complete fire fighter's outfit. The three party crashers didn't have any costumes; they just wore street clothes, and looked like they had come to cause trouble. What made the moment so surreal was Kevin's costume.

He later described it as a, "Monkey Baby," and Sid watched as Kevin confronted the three intruders and ordered them out of his house. He wore only a rubber monkey mask and a large diaper with a safety pin in the front. Kevin was thin and wiry, with muscles honed by manual labor. But the drunk yelling into his face had at least fifty pounds on him. Kevin pointed at the door and said firmly, "Get the fuck out!"

The bigger man responded by putting both hands on Kevin's bare chest and shoving him hard backwards. While Kevin took a step back to regain balance, the drunk left himself exposed with both arms fully extended. Seeing the opening, Joneser cocked his fist back and drilled it into the man's temple. The man's arms went rigid and he fell flat on his face, like a drawbridge coming down. All eyes went to Joneser, whose face twisted into a mask of pain as he used his good hand to gently cup the other.

The unconscious man on the floor let out a wheezing sound and his two friends kneeled down to help him. One looked up to Kevin and all the malice had drained from his face. He now looked like a scared little boy. "I'm really sorry about this," he tried to explain, "Darin just gets drunk and tries to start shit."

Still wearing the monkey mask, Kevin said, "I don't care man, just get him the hell out of here." The men each took an arm and lifted Darin upright as he made small sputtering noises. No one said anything as they dragged him out the door and into the night. As they were leaving, Joneser slipped back to the kitchen where Jenny filled a bag of ice for him and Pete made a quick assessment of his damaged hand.

As the tension left the room, Kevin took off his mask and ran a hand through his short blond hair. He breathed a sigh of relief and sat down with Chrissy. Joneser walked back into the room with the ice on his hand and Jenny at his side. Kevin shook his head with a grin and said to Joneser, "I know you were trying to help, but I was just getting ready to go monkey style on that dude." The others laughed, but no one doubted that Kevin had been ready to come up swinging if Joneser hadn't blindsided the bigger man. Both Kevin and

Joneser had exhibited what they were capable of when pushed to the edge.

The adrenaline rush fizzled out of everyone and exhaustion began to creep in. It was nearing three and time to call it a night, a wild, bizarre, night.

Pete, Cliffy and Sid helped the hosts perform a light cleanup on the house as the other guests filed out. Then they too thanked Kevin and Chrissy, bid them goodnight, and walked outside. As they were getting their bikes, up rolled Arliss, he had wiped off his face paint from earlier in the night. "Hey guys, how'd this party go? Did I miss anything crazy?"

Sid looked at Cliffy, then back at Arliss and replied, "Man, you don't even know. I'll let them tell you the story inside, but just know that Kevin is THE MAN"

"Yeah dude, seriously, your roommate kicks ass." Cliffy added solemnly.

"Alrighty then," said Arliss registering the sincerity in their voices, "I'll see you guys around then." And he headed inside. Cliffy and Sid made their way slowly home, passing other partiers in deteriorating costumes. Sid had taken off the troublesome cape, and Cliff wore only the bunny ears. As they rode, they realized it was much colder than earlier. By the time they reached the Whispering Pines and parked their bikes in the bike rack, the first flakes of snow had begun to fall. They went inside and found Johnny passed out, but no Joneser. They couldn't remember when he left the A frame, but figured he'd find his way home. Later, sometime before dawn, he noisily entered the apartment and made his way to bed.

5.

It seemed as if the whole town slept late the next morning and by nine a.m. some streets still didn't even have tire tracks through the three inches of fresh snow. The boys were in the living room when Joneser awoke and climbed down from his loft. He sat down, and the others cringed when they first saw his face. The red streaks of face paint ran down as before, but now they smeared with blue paint and formed a dark purple where to two blended. The dark colors made his lower face look like a giant bruise. He obviously didn't realize his face looked like this. Cliffy was the first to put it all together and asked, "So, things went well with Smurfette? She seemed nice"

Joneser responded coyly, "I just walked her home, and we hung out for a little bit."

Johnny raised an eyebrow and looked at him incredulous, "Man, you should go look in the mirror."

They rested and recovered all morning, Joneser kept icing his hand, but decided he hadn't done any serious damage. In the afternoon, Cliff and Johnny started preparing for work. Cliffy would swap out a bus with the day driver and begin his four to midnight shift. He followed a route that meandered to several stops around town and then brought riders to the base of the ski area. It was funny that someone who crashed a bicycle as often as he did was capable of operating a bus, but he pulled it off with ease. Plus he was very sociable and enjoyed talking to the locals or offering guidance to the tourists.

While Cliffy was sitting in a warm comfortable seat, drinking coffee and chatting with passengers, Johnny was performing a much more brutal task. Johnny was starting his second year as a snowmaker. For the next few months, he would work ten hour shifts through the coldest nights, managing the network of hoses and snow guns that help cover the mountain with white stuff. Snowmaking was considered a seasonal job, since operations only ran until coverage was complete. The big draw was that each snowmaker received a season pass for their efforts and could make good money with all the long shifts and overtime.

The snowmakers had one snowcat assigned to their department, but mostly they utilized Polaris Widetrack snowmobiles. These workhorse machines had a backrest for carrying two riders and a cargo rack behind that. Widetracks were designed for working hard and pulling heavy loads. All the snowmaker sleds had additional modifications of a trailer hitch and various sizes of pipe fittings bolted to the cargo rack. This way, lengths of hose could be attached to the fittings with quick couplers and dragged into new positions by the sled.

The sleds were also used to move eight foot tall portable snow guns known as Ratniks. The Ratniks were set in position and then connected to the network of compressed air and water lines that run up the side of each ski run. Each worker on the snowmaking team would manage a series of these guns throughout the night. Constantly checking on each of the Ratniks and adjusting pressures or repositioning the nozzle.

Johnny was running through his normal routine when he had a close call on first week of snowmaking. One bitter cold night, he had a snow gun mounted on skids hooked to his Widetrack and was dragging it up an icy, hardpacked ski run. The machine was nearing the crest and laboring under the weight of the heavy gun skid. Johnny was standing up and leaning forward over the bars trying to keep pressure on the skis. Suddenly the sled lurched and he heard a loud BANG! from under the hood. Then the engine revved to the red line before he could let off the gas. The machine stopped moving forward and he almost fell head first over the bars from the momentum. As his brain registered that forward motion had stopped, it had to quickly recalibrate to accept that he was now, in fact, sliding backwards with the gun skid leading the way.

His first reaction was to grab a hand full of brake and lock up the big track. He tried this and got no response as the machine gained speed down the hill. Johnny was a pretty skilled rider, but he knew that trying to handle an out of control Widetrack being dragged backwards by a snow gun would be futile. Moving quickly, he put both feet to one side and jumped as far as possible. He landed safely and watched the gun and the sled disappear off the trail out of sight. The sound of the impact reverberated through the night air as aluminum, plastic and steel all stopped abruptly by a large tree. The engine stayed running and the beam of the headlight now pointed at an angle up into the trees. He walked to the wreck, made a brief inspection of the damage, and then shook his head in disgust as he shut off the engine.

Once he unhooked his pack from sled's back rest, he reached in and found his walkie-talkie. He called to the shift supervisor to explain what happened. The next day a snowcat pulled the damaged gun and sled back to the shop. The mechanics determined that the jack shaft had sheared and it was not operator error. When it broke, the driving force as well as the brake had no connection to the track assembly. Since the incident was declared a mechanical error, and not Johnny's fault, he didn't need to take a pee test, and everyone was just grateful he was uninjured.

6.

The snow kept falling and the ski area's opening day came and went. With a new ski season came all the out-of-state cars full of tourists, or 'Gapers' as they were affectionately called. The locals may have been the heart and soul of town, but it was the tourists and their vacation dollars that allowed the town of C.B. to function as it did. It seemed like the majority were from Texas or the East Coast, and most of them came for a week or more at a time.

Some of the locals, particularly new arrivals, held resentment against the tourists. They whined about them packing the restaurants, flailing down the ski runs or crowding the buses.

But, the boys accepted them as a necessary addition to life in town. As a bus driver, Cliffy interacted every day with the tourists. He explained bus schedules to them, recommended restaurants, told them what ski runs they would enjoy and basically acted as a helpful tour guide. This served the dual purpose of earning him tips and also steering the tourists away from local only spots like certain bars, and basically the whole back side of the mountain.

Sid and the others actively tried to be helpful to lost gapers as well. This could mean giving directions or helping them buy beer, well, buy the right beer. Colorado liquor law had a quirk that limited grocery stores to sell only 3.2 % alcohol beer. Locals knew this and only bought beer at the liquor store, but often Sid would be getting some groceries and see a group of tourists unknowingly stocking up for their Colorado vacation with a cart full of 3.2 beer. He felt it was his obligation to inform them of this common mistake and they were always grateful. Sid felt he had done his civic duty by insuring that people, who had just arrived at high altitude, would receive the full strength alcohol they deserved.

By mid-November the ski area was open, but not all of it. Natural snowfall with the help of Johnny and the other snowmakers had covered most of the blue and green runs on the frontside of the mountain. The steep, rocky chutes of the backside still remained closed though. It was a Saturday and those limited runs would be crowded with early season skiers. That is why the boys needed to go backcountry; they needed to go to Irwin.

Irwin was located twelve miles out of town on a dirt road that closed each winter. The road remained accessible only by snowcat, sled or a few sick bastards who snowshoed or cross country skied out on it. In the late 1800's the town of Irwin was a bustling mining town, with saloons, houses and hotels built up around the mine. Then it all vanished, except for some stone foundations and abandoned mineshafts. In the 1970's the first new residents started buying property on old mining claims and building off-the-grid houses on the old town site. They created a community of about twenty cabins, each unique and varying in its modern amenities. Power came from solar panels, wind turbines, and gas generators. Water was supplied from wells and cisterns. And each home was heated with a woodburning stove or from large propane tanks filled each summer. Some of the larger cabins had flushing toilets with septic tanks, while the smaller cabins had outhouses or hand crank, composting toilets.

Two miles past the town site, sitting majestically at 10,700 ft was the massive Irwin Lodge. Sometimes employees tried to convince guests that the lodge was the setting for Kubrick's 'Shining', but it wasn't true. In fact, the Irwin Lodge was far more isolated than the Stanley Hotel in Estes Park, the movie's actual location. From the Stanley a guest can look out at the T-shirt shops in town, but from the lodge you are gazing at the jagged Anthracite Range of the Rocky Mountains with deep forest all around you. Through the winter the lodge served as a cat skiing operation and in the summer it hosted hikers, fishermen and horseback riding vacationers.

The cat skiing operation involved loading a dozen skiers and a few highly trained guides into the back of specially designed snowcats and driving them up to the top of Scarps ridge. Once there the snowcats could drive along the ridge in either direction accessing acres of ski terrain. When they reached the right spot, the skiers would unload with their guides and ski down through deep, ungroomed powder. The snowcat would meet them at the bottom and they would do it again. When the day was done the skiers would enjoy gourmet dinner and accommodations at the lodge. The lodge also had a legendary bar that was a destination for snowmobilers coming up from town.

The people who owned or rented homes in the town site were self-reliant, hardy, and a little bit crazy. Once snow closed the road, they were cut off from police and ambulance service in town. This added to the community's 'Wild West' atmosphere. Parties in the town site could go all night, with fifteen sleds all parked at one cabin and generator powered lights and music cutting into the darkness. Pulling a sled up to the Irwin Lodge bar, there might be two drunken men or women outside fighting in the snow. And if no lodge guests were in the bar, that meant dogs were under the bar tables and a bong was sitting on top. Irwin was like a forbidden moon orbiting the rogue planet of Crested Butte. If C.B. was a few clicks off from normal society, Irwin was a full twist of the dial.

So that is where Joneser and Sid were preparing to ride their sleds early one Saturday morning. The previous week they had filled up the sleds with fresh gas and oil, tensioned the tracks and suspensions, and made sure no mice had chewed on anything crucial. Then they had ridden them up alleys and over a few short stretches of dirt to get them to the main trail head that allowed access to Irwin. The trailhead had parking lots on one side for cars and trucks, then over a hundred sleds were scattered along the hillsides where people left them for easy access to the trails all winter.

They drove to the trailhead and started unloading gear from the car, today was not just a day of sledding; they had bigger plans. Cliffy had to work, but Johnny came along, as did Arliss. The plan was to tow Johnny and Arliss on skis, behind the sleds. Sid and Joneser had their ski boots on and their skis and poles tucked onto the running boards of the sleds. They hoped to find a line they could shuttle, and take turns towing each other up.

Each of them had on a beanie, goggles, and a backpack slung over their shoulders with the stubby handle of a small shovel sticking out. Under each of their jackets they also wore an expensive, but vital piece of hardware, an avalanche beacon. A beacon is a small transmitter/receiver that gives off a radio signal. Everyone starts the day with their beacons sending out the signal. Then, if there was an avalanche, and someone ended up buried, the others would all turn their beacons to receive. The devices could be used to pinpoint the buried skier as quickly as possible and dig them out.

Beacons, like the other avalanche gear, were tools that everyone was glad to have, but hoped they never needed to use, much like a parachute is to a pilot. Surviving in the backcountry meant following the rules; a beacon without a shovel was worthless. Just as a beacon without knowing how to use it, was equally worthless. The guys made games of beacon practice. Often they would bury them in snow banks and race each other to find them, or they would hide someone's beer or wallet somewhere in the apartment, with a transmitting beacon, and just toss them one on receive. It may not be authentic real world prctice, but finding a beacon under a pile of clothes in the closet still developed the skill. Unfortunately, beacon training was similar to CPR or self-defense training. No one really knew if they could do it until it was absolutely needed. Hours of dedicated practice wouldn't mean anything if you froze in a panic.

Sid pumped the primer of his Skidoo Summit 500 then gave a hard pull on the starter rope; it coughed once and died. He pulled again and the two-stroke engine roared to life in a cloud of blue smoke. Joneser's Polaris XLT 700 took a few more pulls and some messing with the choke. Soon, it too was idling in a cloud of smoke. The engine in the Skidoo was built in Austria and sounded like an instrument of engineering precision and high performance. While the Polaris was proudly built in the USA, and it sounded like three rabid demons trying to claw their way out of an aluminum cage.

Both sleds had paddles on the tracks that allowed them to float through deep powder and climb steep hills. Other modifications designated both machines as pure mountain sleds, not trail sleds. Much like comparing the attributes of a street motorcycle and a dirt bike, no one machine can do it all. To be really good in one situation meant you lost capabilities in another. Mountain sleds could wind their way up through a deep untracked forest, or climb an exposed windblown face. Off trail they had a clear advantage. But riding them at high speed on a smooth fast trail was not their intended purpose. They had a habit of drifting through corners unsteadily, with one ski in the air. On a trail, the rider is not so much driving the sled, as just pointing it in a general direction and hoping for the best.

The crew started out of the parking area slowly, but then began to pick up speed. The main road was traveled by so many snowmobiles that it developed tall bumps or "whoops" that went on for miles and were especially bad near corners. Most riders dealt with whoops by riding slowly through them, the sled rising and falling over each mound like a small boat on rough seas. It *was* possible to try to go full speed through them just skimming over the top, but this was extremely rough on a sled and left the rider barely in control.

Eventually the valley opened up and there was space on the sides of the road they could ride. The paddles on the tracks of the sleds threw chunks of ice and snow out behind it called "roost." Arliss and Johnny avoided this by carving their skis over and staying out from directly behind the sleds. The skiers had squeezed their poles together and slipped them into loops at the end of the towropes. Now they stood upright with their arms in front of them holding the classic pose of a water skier. When the sleds dropped off the trail and sped across a field the skiers crouched and used their knees to absorb the bumps. While the concept was the same as water skiing, towing behind the sleds carried a bit more risk. The speed was constantly changing and catching an edge could easily blow out a knee.

Along the way they passed other sledders and large groups of rental sleds. Further up the snowy road they noticed something out of place. From a distance it looked like a large box tilting off the side of the road, then as they got closer it became obvious is was a vehicle of some sort. It wasn't uncommon for some fool in a 4x4 to drive between the ROAD CLOSED signs and try to make it up the trail, but no one ever made it several miles in where this thing sat.

As they pulled up to it, they realized it was a late nineteen eighties Ford van, and in place of wheels, it had four large track assemblies. It became obvious that the machine was traveling along the hard packed snow of the road, heading for the lodge, but then it got too close to the edge. Once the left side tracks slide off the road, the machine dug a deep trench into the soft snow. Now, the van sat at a steep angle with the driver's side buried in the snow. A sled was parked next to the stuck van with two men scrambling around and tentatively poking a shovel underneath it to assess the best course of action.

"Need a hand?" Joneser called out. A guy in greasy, dark blue coveralls turned away from the front axle he was reaching for, and looked up at Joneser with disdain.

"Yeah", he replied with dripping sarcasm, "You push, and I'll gun it, ok?"

The other guy, wearing snowmobile bibs and an Irwin Lodge employee jacket walked over to Sid and Joneser as they killed the engines on the sleds. Arliss and Johnny were still behind at the ends of the tow ropes. They took the opportunity to stretch their arms and legs.

"What is this thing?" asked Sid, "I mean besides a giant ass van with monster tracks under it."

"It's called the MATRAX. It's something new the lodge is trying out this year. I'm Dan by the way," he said as he shook hands with Sid and Joneser. They introduced themselves and asked if he was the driver.

"Yeah, I was coming up yesterday afternoon with a full load of guests who had just flown in. The lodge is trying this thing instead of picking them up in a snowcat because it can do the run twice as fast with half the gas. But, obviously it's not perfect as you can see. I was doing great, then this big group of tour sleds freaked out when I caught up to them. They just stopped, blocking half the trail, I thought I had room to sneak by them, but once the tracks were even close to the edge it just slipped off and kept going. I turn up toward the trail and floored it." Dan was trying hard not to laugh as he recalled the scene. Sid and Joneser smiled as they pictured it. "It seemed for a second like it was going to climb back on to the trail, so I stayed in it. The tourists on the sleds were all shitting their pants, my guests in the van all thought we could make it so they start cheering me on! Then it just went right over. It was pretty violent, some people banged their heads and shit."

"How fast does this thing go?" asked Joneser.

"Oh, it'll do forty. It's got a big block," Dan answered.

"HEY," came a sharp yell from Phillip, the mechanic. "Can you give him a ride to the lodge?"

"Sure," replied Sid.

"Great!" Phillip continued, "Dan, go get the work cat, that way I can keep the sled and I won't be stuck out here." Phillip was visibly annoyed, but it appeared to be directed at the machine or perhaps the situation. It was obvious he and Dan got along well, and this was probably just a normal day for the lodge.

Dan, climbed on behind Sid, Johnny and Arliss picked up the tow lines, and they rode the last few miles until the green metal roof of the lodge came into view. Sid drove right up to the main entrance where two cabin cats were idling as guests loaded skis into boxes on the back and climbed the aluminum folding stairs up into the cabin. A couple of the ski guides were standing there watching as Sid let Dan off the sled. Dan thanked him and walked away. The guides immediately saw what the boys were planning and walked over to Sid. They were a man and a woman in their thirties and wore maroon one-piece ski suits with lodge logos. His suit had an embroidered script that read *Stu*, while her's spelled *Carrie*. "You guys know what you're doing out here?" asked Stu. "Where do you plan to ski?"

Stu spoke with the authority of a policeman leaning in a car window. He got paid to help out-of-shape rich people find fresh powder runs they could tell stories about back home. These professional guides were experts in avalanche forecasting and control. They monitored every layer of the snowpack and used explosives and other means to trigger slides that could potentially kill those out-of-shape rich people. Sid had respect for the senior guides, and appreciated any information he might glean from them.

"We want to make laps from that old mine under Mt. Owen, work our way along the shelf and skirt around the cliffs." Sid spoke to them honestly and with confidence. He didn't want to appear like an inexperienced goofball who had no right coming to the backcountry. The guides were obviously sizing up the crew, looking over their equipment and considering the area they intended to ski. As the closest emergency personnel, the guides felt obligated to assist in serious injuries or rescues near the lodge property. However, this took them away from paying customers, and they would rather avoid this at all costs.

Stu looked across the basin at the general area Sid had described and thought for a moment. Carrie turned to him and said, "Those cliffs have been sluffing all week, anything that was going to go probably would have." They both turned back to Sid. Stu smiled and said, "That sounds like a good spot for today, just don't try to huck any cliffs. The base isn't deep enough yet. One of our employees dropped a ten footer here last week and broke his femur."

"Oh, shit," said Sid with genuine empathy, "Is he ok?"

"Yeah he's healing now, but he rode forty minutes in back of a cat to the trailhead screaming while we pulled traction on him. It was pretty awful." Stu's face had gone grim as the recent memory came back, but he cleared it away and perked up. "So be careful out there, and don't die!"

"Ok, thanks for the insight," Sid smirked as he pulled his start rope and turned the sled back to the entrance of chute parking lot. Arliss and Johnny had walked over to Joneser as they waited. Sid pulled up and Joneser asked, "Did the almighty mountain pope give us his blessing?"

"Yeah man, he's cool," Sid nodded.

"That's Stu Weston," Arliss said. "He was ski patrol before this. I think he's pretty legit."

"Yeah I think he just wanted to make sure we weren't here to ski Ruby chute or some other crazy shit," Sid agreed.

"Alright, let's hit it then, we're burnin' a bluebird day!" Joneser called out. He was getting anxious for some turns, which was certainly understandable. Sid looked up and realized that the morning cloud cover had blown off and indeed there was not a cloud in the sky. Since they had climbed a few hundred feet up to the lodge, and now they were going back down, the two skiers kicked off over a snow bank and disappeared down the hill. Joneser and Sid raced the sleds down the switch-backed road and caught them at the bottom. They dropped the towropes and the skiers grabbed on as they headed into Robinson basin. The plan was to ride into the big open basin, look up at the face they planned to hit and scope the lines. Also they were dropping off food, water and extra layers at the rendezvous point where skiers and sleds would meet after each run.

They made their way through the forested entrance into the basin, and soon it opened up to vast walls of snow in three directions around them. Straight ahead to the north lay the knife edged barrier of Scarps Ridge, to the east was a face leading up onto the lodge's property, and to the west was the aspect they planned to ski. They killed the engines and looked up at the steep exposed face in front of them and marveled at the single sled track that started at the bottom, climbed straight up the ridiculously steep slope, zig zagged around rocks, and then continued to climb up to within a few feet of the rocky crest. At the top it made an arcing turn and descended the same steep slope, cut to the side and threaded down a chute barely twice the width of the sled. The more they looked around at other tracks, the more they realized they were looking at the work of a master sled rider. The artistry was visible in the way the track sidehilled across the top of a wide cliff face, looped around a small rock and then came back across the face. It was someone who had complete trust in their machine and their own abilities. One sputter from the sled or one moment of hesitation and both rider and sled would be tumbling down the slope.

The boys were still commenting on the tracks when the sound of a nasty two stroke echoed through the basin like an approaching monster. It sounded like it was coming from directly above them and they all looked up in time to see a sled come blasting between some trees and over the edge of a cornice. It sailed far out into the air then started to drop. The rider tapped the brake, and the skis dove down until they matched the exact angle of the slope rushing closer. Powder flowed over the nose of the machine as it gently landed in the pocket of deep snow. Then with an unholy roar, it tore through the snow, carved with one ski high in the air and pulled up next to the guys. It was the same model Polaris as Joneser's. But, it was modified and obviously had performance pipes on the exhaust because, even idling, it sounded like a rapidly firing cannon with one explosion leading into the next. The rider hit the red kill button on his handlebars and started to undo his helmet strap.

He pulled off his battered motocross fullface helmet revealing short, blond hair bleached by the sun. The man smiled broadly and crow's feet appeared at the corners of his eyes. His face had a few days of stubble. He wore black insulated snow pants and an old black leather snowmobile-racing jacket with two red stripes down each arm. The guys all knew instantly they were looking into the face of Irwin legend, John Rippey. Some even called him the mayor of Irwin. He glanced at each of them and said, "Well, you guys sure picked a nice day to live in Colorado!"

Joneser greeted him, "Hey Rip, we should have known those were your tracks." The older man looked at Joneser for a moment, and then recognized him from a local bar frequented by the town's old guard. He snapped his gloved fingers and said, "Hey, I've met you at Cadaver's before."

"Yeah, man, how's it going?" Joneser introduced the others to Rippey, and they made some small talk. The guys had all heard the basic story that he had moved out to Irwin in the seventies, built a cabin in the town site with a big workshop, and made money repairing sleds. People would often bring machines up from town for him to fix and he worked for cash or barter. He also volunteered hundreds of hours on the local search and rescue team and had helped to locate lost hikers in the summer and injured snowmobilers in the winter. A permanent sunglass tan ringed his eyes and his skin looked tough and weathered from decades of exposure to high altitude elements. He was in his fifties and incredibly fit. His sharp mind always offered a clever line or some deeper insight, making him captivating to listen to.

The guys sorted out their gear, making sure their beacons were transmitting. Rippey offered to lead them up the best route for shuttling. He also suggested they shorten the tow lines to ten feet since they would be on tighter trails and it would be easier to control the sleds. That done, they rode off with Rippey's monster triple leading the way. Soon they came to a hundred–year-old wooden structure of thick timbers and iron brackets located next to a large pit. This was one of the many old mines left over from the gold boom. Rippey flashed a 'hang loose' gesture with thumb and pinky extended from his fist, then gunned his engine and disappeared in a quick puff of two-stroke smoke.

Joneser and Sid stowed the tow lines and removed their skis and poles from the sleds as Johnny and Arliss tightened up boots and adjusted goggles. "That was cool seeing Rippey." Arliss said.

"Yeah, that guy's awesome, I can't believe some of those lines he takes with that sled," Johnny responded.

"Maybe that's just how it is riding a sled out here for as long as he has," Joneser considered, "You either get really good or die."

"Well, on that note." CLICK, Johnny snapped his other boot into his binding and stood up straight. He punched both of his mittened fists together and bounced up and down radiating excitement. The skiers poled through the untracked snow towards the slope and the sleds made their way back down the same path they had come up, hoping to pack it down and make it nice and firm. The better the trail got the less fuel it would take for each run. The skiers beat the sleds to the bottom by about five minutes; they were both grinning like Jokers and cleaning snow from their hats and goggles. "That good huh?" Sid asked with glee. The euphoric buzz that held the skiers was highly contagious. "DDDDDUUUUUUDDDDEEE!!" was all Arliss could manage in return.

"So much pow," was Johnny's assessment. Small clumps of snow hung from his beard, and bobbed as he spoke. The two explained that the run starts with a mellow flowy run through nicely spaced glades, then it quickly gets steeper and the trees start to get tighter. Be ready, Arliss said, because the tree line ends and you have about 10 more feet of steep before the cliff band. The snow between the trees and the cliff is windblown so you either come out in a drift or on a hard smooth icy section. Cut to skier's left and there is a gap in the cliffs. Come through there and it's big powder carves to the bottom.

"Right on," Sid grinned, "Safety meeting?" The others agreed with enthusiasm and he fished from his pocket a small brass pipe and a purple lighter. He slid open the cover on the Proto Pipe and twisted open a tubular compartment. From this he shook some loose weed into the bowl and stirred it with the thin poker. Then he slid the compartment and the poker back onto the pipe forming a complete unit. The pipe made it around the circle twice, then they fired up the sleds and headed back to the mine. This time, Joneser and Sid stepped into their skis as the other two rode the sleds down. Smoking weed and skiing was so commonplace that none of them ever gave it much thought. The buzz helped ease sore muscles and seemed to amplify the experience. Everything seemed faster, steeper, deeper and just more fun.

Sid pulled his skis from the snow and separated the two. He took a quick glance at the bases and reviewed the condition. Long jagged gouges stretched down the center of each ski, but they had been filled with black Ptex that contrasted against the opaque base. Three inches of inner metal edge on one ski had been torn away, that gap was filled back in with grey JB weld. *Tools not jewels*, Sid thought as he dropped each ski flat on the snow. The mantra held that skis are not to be cherished for display, they are to be used however necessary to reach fresh lines. He then lifted each boot and tapped it with his ski pole twice to knock snow off the bottom before stepping into his bindings. Seven years ago his Lange X9 boots had been top of the line race boots, the stiffest boots available. Now, they felt as soft and comfortable as a pair of Converse high tops. One boot had two mismatched buckles, and he had taken a Sharpie marker to them adding designs and slogans. The left side toe read 'Feel the Flow' and on the right, an homage to Lane Meyer that read 'Go that way, really fast.'

Sid followed Joneser into the woods. The weed had been a bit of a creeper high, and his head started to swim with THC and adrenaline. He felt a disconnect between his body and his mind. Sid pictured a fighter pilot, decked out in full flight suit and helmet settling into a tiny cockpit, with Sid's Smith goggles as his viewport.

The pilot was controlling this high performance mountain mech as it gathered speed and started carving around trees. Sensors in the legs gathered input on the snow conditions and varied the angle of the body and skis for maximum speed and control. Flight monitoring systems detected a variance in consistency between snow in the shadow, and snow in the sun, then quickly recalibrated to the changes. The mission's directive was to lay tracks across as much powder as possible, with bonus points awarded for deeper sections of pow. The pilot avoided 'target fixation' by always looking at the gap between the trees, and never directly at the trees themselves. Looking at a tree could draw you right into it.

Like Pac-man gobbling up dots, Sid tore through the woods, his ski tips slicing up fresh lines. Every few turns he caught a glimpse of Joneser in his peripheral, or heard a WHOOOP! of joy from his partner.

His skis sank into the untracked powder and snow billowed up onto his chest and face every few turns. Soft, mushroom-shaped pillows concealing buried stumps and rocks loomed in his path. Sid bounced off the top of each mound and landed deep in the white room as snow splashed onto his goggles and he quickly brushed it off with a swipe of his glove. Evergreen boughs brushed his jacket as he ducked and swerved through the forest.

Just as the others had warned them, the terrain started to pitch forward and got steeper. Simultaneously, the trees seemed to close in and become denser. Sid cut over next to Joneser and they both eased to a stop right as the trees ended. They cautiously glided out from the trees and saw nothing but a horizon line ahead of them. Beyond that, a half mile away was the opposing wall of the basin, but in front of them the earth just seemed to end as the slope rolled out of sight. They started cutting left and found they could traverse quite easily. And just like Johnny had said, they skated over sections that were windblown to the point of being icy and sections of deep drifts that they sometimes had to step through.

They came to the gap in the cliff band and analyzed the tracks the other two had made, trying to get a read on the consistency. Johnny and Arliss had alternated their turns over each other creating perfectly stitched figure eights down the face. Small chunks stuck up here and there indicating debris from an avalanche that had fallen a week ago. "After you my good sir," Joneser said as he bowed and rolled his hand in a formal invitation. Sid didn't have to be asked twice, and he dropped in laying out a series of arcing turns. He dragged his hand through the soft snow as it billowed up to hit him in the face. A feeling of ecstasy gripped him as he made his final turns and coasted to a stop at the bottom. The growl of two stroke engines echoed into the basin and grew louder as the two machines broke from the trees and raced up to Sid. They killed the engines and immediately the valley was silent again except for the 'tink, tink' sound of hot metal expanding and the 'tsssssss,' 'tsssssss' sound of snow dripping onto it.

Just as they looked up, Joneser dropped into the slope, he pushed his skis into a wedge shape for just a moment, as if it was his first time down the bunny hill. Then he pulled them parallel and it became clear that he did not intend to make any turns. He stood up his full 6'2" and extended his arms out to both sides. He gained velocity like a bullet, but he had chosen a line that missed every chunk of icy debris. Despite his accelerating speed, nothing made him deviate from a perfectly straight line between point A and point B.

The others started cheering for him and laughing ecstatically. This was a move they had only seen in ski movies, done by pros in Alaska and Europe. They didn't know their friend was capable of 'straightlining' a big face. He made it all the way down the slope and sailed up to them so fast he was able to carve hard at the last minute and throw a wave of snow on to them. They all high fived him and congratulated him on a 'sick' line. Arliss looked up at the tracks and declared, "Let's do it again!"

And so it went for the next few hours. They made more laps, then took a break for lunch, then made some more laps. As they chewed up the lines closer to the gap they kept moving skier's right to find fresh tracks, this meant a longer traverse over to the gap. It also meant the height of the cliff band grew the farther over they went. Close to the gap it was only about ten feet high, but now when they came out of the trees they were over a cliff of black rock that stood fifty feet high.

Someone suggested another smoke break and Sid reloaded the Proto Pipe. He dug the purple lighter out of his pocket and found it packed with snow. Discouraged, he tried several times to light it, but with a wet flint, it was not happening. Johnny pulled a white lighter from his coat and gave it a flick, the diamond shaped flame danced out of the top. Sid reached for it, and then Joneser solemnly said, "Dude, white lighters are bad luck."

"Whatever," Johnny retorted, "I say a lighter that won't light is bad luck."

Arliss mocked Joneser and asked, "Aren't you the guy who lifts your feet every time you're riding in a car that crosses railroad tracks?"

"Yeah, but that's for good luck," he responded.

Sid blew out a big hit and asked, "Wow, man, did you buy your book of spells from an ad in the back of High Times?"

"Fine, laugh it up. And it's called a grimoire, by the way. A book of spells is a grimoire." Joneser relented as he used the white lighter despite the dark omen.

Sid had to get in one more chop and said, "I would totally keep making fun of you Gandalf, if you hadn't shown us all up with that dope figure eleven." Joneser silently nodded as he smiled a shit-eating grin, but his raised eyebrows said, "That's right motherfucker!"

Sid and Joneser dropped into the woods again. The snow was starting to thicken into the consistency of mashed potatoes, and Sid was starting to feel a little off. His legs were getting tired, and cloud cover had rolled in, making the light in the trees tricky. Still, the lure of fresh tracks drew him further to the right, while Joneser went left and followed a path he had previously taken. Sid had found a section where the trees seemed really spread out. He used the opportunity to make fewer turns and give his legs a break. Making less turns saved energy, but his speed quickly increased. When the slope became steeper he suddenly pictured himself shooting straight out over the cliff. His body reacted instinctively and dug his edges in hard. The skis bit into a tight carve that scrubbed all his speed and arced back up the slope some. He was panting and his legs quivered as he held on to a tree and gathered himself. *This was dumb*, he thought. *If those guys want more that's fine, but after this, I'm done.*

He had to walk a little way in the deep powder to get going again as he slowly made his way down, using the 'snowplow' maneuver to check his speed. Sid wasn't even trying to make nice powder turns any more, just simple and sloppy survival turns. He started cutting back to the left so he would have less of a traverse. In front of him he could see where it got brighter at the edge of the trees, and he spotted a gap he could use to exit. Two pine trees formed an opening the size of a doorway with a bushy pine bough hanging down off the right side tree. Sid couldn't wait to get out of these trees. He brought his skis together to get through, increasing speed, but he knew he could brake again as soon as he was clear. He put his shoulder out to push the tree branch away from his face and...POW!

The impact rocked him like a check from an NHL player. He was spun backwards and watched his view rapidly blur as he tumbled end over end. Terror gripped him like a crushing fist. Survival instinct overrode any cognitive thought. When his back hit the snow the second time, the tail of his right ski jammed hard through the crusty wind pack and stuck. His other ski had released and his free leg flopped to the snow,

The impact knocked the wind out of him. He breathed in a shallow breath and let it out slowly with a long low groan. The crash had happened so fast, Sid needed a moment to assess the situation and to let the adrenaline dissipate. His goggles were full of snow and had slid down over his nose, the frames half covering both eyes. Trying not to move more than toes and fingers, he determined nothing was seriously injured, but his shoulder throbbed like it had been hit with a wooden baseball bat.

That soft branch hanging down must have concealed a broken off stub of a much thicker branch. *I'm lucky it wasn't pointing at me*, he thought, then he reconsidered. *Maybe being impaled on a tree up there would be better than where I am. So, where am I?* He could tell he was lying on his back at a steep angle downwards hanging from his right leg. Slowly he brought his arm over and lifted the goggles off his face, the strap slipped off with his beanie, he let them go and he heard the goggles skitter down the crusty snow. He calculated that he heard the goggles slide about seven or eight feet before the sound stopped. *Did they come to a stop on a nice wide ledge, or did they plummet off the cliff?* Above him he could see only sky, he craned his head as far as he could over his shoulder, hoping to see one last tree or a rocky outcrop and just saw the icy slope fall away out of sight.

Next, he started to pull his elbows in underneath him to prop himself up and try to look uphill, but the ski that was anchoring him tore into the snow and he slipped down about an inch. He quickly spread his arms back out for more surface contact, he remembered some rock climber dude going on about 'smearing' himself against the rock for more friction to hang on. Sid tried to 'smear' as much contact against the snow as possible and thought that rock climber had been really annoying at the time. He also tried to angle the tip of his ski up hill, so the tail bit in like a barb, but something about that made it worse, and he started to slide again. *This was it, he was going to fall backwards off a cliff onto his head. His parents would be distraught and the Irwin guides would be pissed.* NO!NO!NO!NO!NO!...then he stopped sliding. A fresh wave of panic washed over him and with fear in his voice he yelled "FUCK!" then, "HEYYY! HEEELLLPPP!" then he listened but didn't hear an answer. Shit! He did hear something though, a sled, goddamn it! With a sled coming into the basin no one will ever hear him, and even if it is Arliss and Johnny, neither of those sleds could climb this slope and make it up the steep pitch between the cliffs.

But, it wasn't either of those sleds. It was something much louder and more powerful, definitely piped. And it was flying; the sled sounded like it was full throttle as the roar reverberated off the opposite wall of the basin. The noise seemed to be getting closer. Sid closed his eyes and tried to triangulate the location of the sound. He listened to the roar of exhaust crescendo as the machine made a straight line up the face they had been skiing. He heard the two-stroke engine ease up slightly as the rider expertly feathered the throttle, paused and then gassed it some more. Sid knew what he was hearing but still couldn't believe it. He figured the machine had started to loose traction at the peak of its straight up attack. Typically a rider would arc their sled back down the hill in a move called 'high marking', but this guy wasn't heading back down. He had tipped the sled onto its uphill side and was leaning into the mountain as he balanced the sled on one ski and worked the thumb throttle, giving it as much gas as possible without spinning the track.

'Side hilling,' as it's known, allowed a sled to get up a steeper slope than just going straight at it. However, it took incredible skill and commitment, one wrong move and the sled could get stuck or worse, tumble down the mountain gaining speed and shedding parts like a meteor burning up in the atmosphere. Sid was stunned when he heard the sled crest the pinnacle of the climb, then it slowly worked its way through the trees in his direction. It stopped twenty feet uphill from where he was and he heard someone rapidly crunching through the snow. Sid knew it could only be one person coming to his rescue, and a second later he heard Rippey's reassuring voice say, "Don't fall now, 'cause I'm not diving for you."

With the confidence of a mountaineer he stomped down the slope making sure each footprint dug deep into the crust. Sid tensed as he made the last few steps to him, fearing that his anchor would let loose before Rippey reached him, but an instant later he felt the old mechanic's hand clamp onto his boot like a vise grip. Sid blurted out "Oh my god, thank you, I thought I was going to die."

"Well, you will," Rippey responded without missing a beat, "and I can't help you with that, but I think you're safe for today."

They said little else while Rippey eased Sid back up the slope. Once he was safe, they popped his boot from the binding. He scooted back a little more and stood up. He was overcome with gratitude, and tears started to well up in his eyes as he hugged Rippey. Sid had kept his cool while he dangled upside down, but now he could acknowledge the full realization that he had been mere feet from certain death. Emotion overtook him and he shuddered as Rippey patted his back with reassurance. When Sid composed himself, Rippey pointed him up the hill to his sled and told him he'd gather his gear. The snowmobiling boots that Rippey wore had much better traction than Sid's ski boots. And he was able to walk down to the edge of the cliff and retrieve the lost goggles and hat that had come to rest on the thin edge of stone. Then he hiked back up and grabbed both skis on the way.

He found Sid sitting on the seat of his sled. He'd unzipped his jacket and pulled the sleeve down off his shoulder, a deep bruise was already forming where he had hit the branch. As Rippey walked up Sid looked up at him and asked in amazement, "How the hell, did you ever know I was up there? What do you have spider sense, or something?"

Rippey grinned, "Not quite. I was just coming down from the lodge and thought I'd see how you guys made out. I watched your buddy come screaming through that gap, so I waited to see someone else go. Then here you come with your gymnastics tumbling routine."

"That is unbelievable. I mean, that's like a fucking miracle, that you saw me."

"Well," Rippey's smile grew wider, "sometimes I'm just at the right place at the right time." His smile dimmed, and he added, "I've also been at the wrong place at the wrong time, so it balances out."

The others had gathered down the hill and were yelling up at them, asking what happened. From below, they couldn't have seen any of the crash or recovery. "Time to tell those guys you're ok," Rippey said, putting a hand on Sid's good shoulder. "You're ok, right?" Sid pulled his coat back into place and stood up. He had gained his composure, but his eyes were still slightly red.

He looked directly at Rippey and said, "I will never forget this for as long as I live, and if I ever have a chance to help you in any way, I swear I will." Rippey nodded. He knew the oath was genuine and the gratitude was sincere, but he also knew the transient nature of ski towns and ski bums. This kid might not even be here at the end of the season. Still, it seemed like a powerful moment and Rippey didn't want to blow the kid off, so he responded.

"I guess you'll know it when I need it. Are you ok to make it down the hill?"

Sid dropped his skis on the snow, "Yeah, man, I think I'm good." He stepped in and started shuffling to the gap, and then he cautiously made his way down with short controlled turns. He was greeted by cheers from his friends and a bear hug from Joneser that took him to the ground. Pain flared in his bruised shoulder, but it was worth it to be among the living and celebrating a successful day in the mountains. They heard Rippey's sled fire up above them and start maneuvering back through the trees, it shot down the gap and came pulling up next to them. When he shut off the engine the others all shook his hand and thanked him for saving Sid. Arliss asked if they could buy him some drinks at the lodge bar and he declined, saying, "I was already up there for too long today, but you could put it towards my tab if you feel like it."

The sun had fallen past the western ridge and the basin filled with shadow. Rippey stepped off his sled and opened the small compartment in the seat. As he reached inside Sid noticed TEAM YAMAHA stitched into the padded lower section of Rippey's vintage jacket. The older man pulled out a water bottle, took a long swig and said, "Well, if you boys don't need me for anything else, then I think I'll get going. And if you plan on heading to the lodge, try to stay out of trouble. I think you've had enough close calls for one day."

They thanked him again and began preparing to leave. Right before he pulled away, Rippey caught Sid's eye and gave him a knowing wink, then he gunned his sled and disappeared into the trees. Johnny said "I think beers at the bar are a great idea 'cause," he looked at Sid, "Lucy, you got some 'splaining to do."

"Yeah, we wanna know just what the fuck happened up there?" Joneser added.

"Alright, alright, let's get up there," Sid said with his hands up in surrender.

"I'm buying the first round," Arliss declared. And with that, they made the short drive back up to the lodge.

7.

Late day clouds had rolled in, and as the sun fell behind the peaks it set them ablaze with reds and purples. Several sleds were sitting in the parking lot when the guys pulled up to the bar at the lodge. Two couples were standing outside watching the sunset. After the crew parked the sleds and reeled in the towlines, they headed into the coatroom and stamped off the snow onto the grated floor. They hung coats and packs on some of the hundreds of coat hangers lining the walls. A metal helmet rack stood off to the side with fullface moto helmets hanging from it. Then they opened the interior door and stepped through into the bar, walking carefully in their ski boots on the wet wooden floor.

More than a dozen people were in the small bar. Some sat at the scattered tables while four guys stood in heated battle at the worn out foosball table. The rest sat on stools at the long wooden bar with a shining brass pipe for a footrest. The guys were greeted warmly by

Thomas the bartender who stood in stark contrast to the grunge look adopted by most of the bartenders in town. In a white buttoned shirt with a black bowtie, he had the class and debonair of Roger Moore's 007. "What can I get started for you guys?" he asked as he swept a washrag across the gleaming surface of the bar and smiled.

The guys moved up to the bar and looked around. In typical arrangement, the top shelf held bottles that were way too expensive, the middle was lined with good name brands and the bottom shelf held swill. Arliss noticed a lack of beer taps and asked Thomas about it. He then explained that despite numerous attempts, it had proven impossible to use kegs reliably at such a high altitude, but he did keep a stock of canned beer in back and listed off some brands. Arliss held up four fingers and said simply, "PBR's please." Before Thomas walked through the back door he added, "We also have some specials if you are feeling fancy," and he pointed with the washrag to a small chalkboard.

In stylish writing the chalkboard read TOP HITS! Funky Cold Medina $4, Brass Monkey $4, Gin and Juice $4, 1 Bourbon 1 Scotch 1 Beer $12. The guys smiled at this as they made their way to a table over by a window. Soon Thomas returned with the beers and they clanked them together over the table in a group cheers.

" Alright. Spill it," Joneser demanded as he leaned in. Sid recounted his story with dramatic flair and then fielded follow-up questions. *No*, he didn't see his life flash before him, *Yes*, he did wonder if his binding might release on him and *No*, if he had died, it didn't mean Johnny got his sled.

The bar continued to fill as sleds pulled up outside and guests from the lodge trickled in to mingle with the locals. Three wealthy businessmen with thick New York accents drank shots from the top shelf, loudly egging each other on and proclaiming how awesome they would ski tomorrow. Sadly, they did not understand the effect high altitude hard drinking would have on new arrivals from sea level. They would be lucky if they made it out for one powder run tomorrow. Several of the ski guides came in including the two Sid had spoken with in the morning. The New Yorkers spotted the guides and bought them a round. The older guide, Stu, recognized Sid and wandered over to their table to ask how the day had gone. Sid reluctantly told him the tale of his near miss as Stu listened intently, when he was done, Stu let out a low whistle and said, "Man you must have some good mountain karma, not to mention the most unlikely guardian angel in Colorado." Then the guide tipped his glass to cheers Sid and walked off. This reminded Sid he was going to contribute to Rippey's tab. He opened his wallet, found a single $20 bill and explained to Thomas what he wanted to do. As he was at the bar talking, it gradually became apparent that a noise could be heard growing louder. Thomas turned down the stereo and quizzically asked Sid, "What the hell is that?"

The din of the bar died down as everyone focused on the roar outside growing closer. Sid was reminded of monster trucks or the street drag racers he had seen in Denver. Someone said, "That's not a snowcat!" Someone else said, "And it's no sled, either." People leaned toward the windows as the glow of headlights breached the darkness. The roar of a V8 engine became absolutely deafening, as the White Ford van on tracks pulled into the exterior light of the lodge. Sid realized that the machine must have torn its exhaust off when it went off the road, and he grinned at the obnoxious display of pure horsepower.

Shortly after, Phillip and Dan entered the bar through the back entrance and received a round of applause and cheers from the lodge employees who knew they had spent all day rescuing the MATRAX. Thomas served them their 'Shiftys,' lodge employees received a shift drink after a full day of work. The driver and mechanic collapsed into two empty chairs next to the guys' table then turned their seats to join them. "Nice work," Joneser said. "You freed the beast!"

"That thing sounds gnarly," Sid added.

Phillip responded, "Yeah when it went off the road it tore most of the exhaust off. I think it sounds awesome!" Everyone agreed that the van sounded fierce, but guests probably wouldn't enjoy the ride.

"Seriously, I would go deaf driving it much further," Dan said. Then, getting an idea, he added, "Hey, you guys want to come up to the lounge?" He held two pinched fingers to his mouth forming the international symbol for smoking a joint. The guys were honored to be invited into the inner sanctum of the lodge.

They paid their tab and Thomas gave them a salute as Phil and Dan led them into the main area of the lodge. They slipped off their ski boots and placed them against the wall. Walking quietly in socks, they passed a massive stone fireplace where guests sat in cozy leather chairs. Then the two employees led them up a wide carpeted staircase to the third floor. A door marked Employees Only opened into a long hallway with small rooms lining one side for employee housing.

Most doors were closed, but they passed one with several employees excitedly playing a video game while a cloud of ganja smoke drifted from the room. The hallway ended at a much larger room with three couches all angled towards an old TV with a VCR underneath it. VHS tapes were stacked next to it and Point Break played on the screen. A few tired lodge workers zoned out after a hard day. These guys and girls worked in the kitchen and housekeeping or as wait staff. Unlike the guides, who made friends with the guests to earn bigger tips, these back-of-the-house workers tended to avoid any interaction with the guests. The lounge was considered a place of quiet refuge, so as the guys entered they were met with a few annoyed glances. Then Phil spoke up and addressed the room, "These guys helped us out today, so I'm burning a joint with them. You are all welcome to join in." This broke the tension and granted the outsiders temporary approval by the others.

A girl who had been resting under a blanket poked her head out and immediately smiled at Joneser. He recognized Jenny, the girl from Halloween, and sat next to her. He learned that she picked up a couple shifts each week at the lodge working as a waitress. Arliss, Johnny and Sid each found seats on the couches as people who had been lounging sat up to make room. The guys were introduced to Ray the head chef. He was a tall Mexican who still wore the white shirt and black pinstriped pants of his uniform. They also met Chad, another cook, and Courtney the day shift bartender. Dan and Phil found seats, and Phil grabbed a POWDER magazine from a pile and got busy using it as a workspace to roll a joint. He broke his weed up into a loose pile, then took a paper from an orange Zig Zag box and sprinkled the weed evenly into the folded paper. He licked the glue strip and rolled the paper over the weed, twisting one end and shaking the half-finished joint to compact the filling. This created space to add even more weed into the open end, then he twisted it shut and performed the final step. He folded a dollar bill around the thick joint and rolled it in the bill until it had a smooth perfectly cylindrical shape. Then he lit it up, took a big puff, passed it to his left and promptly started rolling another one.

As the smoke filled the air, everyone settled in, and the stories began. Phil and Dan recounted their epic fiasco of salvaging the MATRAX. Then Ray and Chad told of how they had narrowly survived the dinner rush. It seems they had run out of the lodge's signature elk steak, so the two formed hamburger into the shape of the steaks and covered them with an extra thick layer of the shitake mushroom sauce. Jenny helped determine which guests would most likely fall for the trick. She explained her criteria, "I went with the three drunkest people and the woman who asked what an elk was." Everyone burst out laughing and couldn't believe it worked. Jenny added, "Two of those New Yorkers got burger and they tipped 40%!"

When the laughter died down, Phil looked at Joneser and asked, "So how was the snow?" Joneser responded with a maniacal grin, "It was an epic day, right up to the point where Sid almost died!" This got everyone's attention. Phil arched his eyebrows significantly and looked over at him while saying, "Ooooohhh?"

Sid was reluctant to replay the whole event so he gave a quick version, "Yeah, I was coming out over the cliffs on the East wall of Robinson and caught a tree branch. It sent me tumbling and I ended up hanging backwards upside down from one ski over the top of the cliffs. It was pretty gnarly. I really thought I was a dead man."

Dan excitedly jumped in and asked the others, "So one of you found him like that?"

Sid continued, "No man, that's the crazy part, he was already down," he motioned to Joneser, "and these two were shuttling the sleds back down."

"So, what happened?" Chad blurted out, the suspense getting to him. Ray punched him in the arm, and snapped at him, "Shut the fuck up and he'll tell us!" All eyes fell on Sid, and he said, "Rippey saved me. He just came out of nowhere, I heard his sled climb up to where I was and then he just walks up and grabs my leg. It was frickin' crazy!"

Everyone let this news sink in for a beat, then Courtney, who had been pretty quiet so far spoke up. "So this had to be afternoon right? Because John was hanging out at my bar for like three hours. He had lunch and a few drinks, then around two he left cash on the bar, blew me a kiss and said he had to get going. Then he just rides off and saves someone's life? That guy is amazing!"

"Well bud, looks like you are the latest addition to Rippey's list of saved lives," Phil said as he put a hand on Sid's shoulder.

"You mean counting the people he's saved while working with search and rescue?" Sid asked.

"Sure, I bet he's saved some lost gapers before, but I mean when he saved half of Irwin's founding population." Everyone leaned in just a bit closer.

Ray lifted an eyebrow and said, "What's this now?"

Phil looked surprised at the faces and addressed everyone in the circle, "So, none of you have heard this one? Oh man, this is like pure Irwin Legend. People like Tony, Janice, Big Ed," Phil counted off fingers on his hand as he dropped names, "uhh, Sven and Susan, they'd all be dead now if it weren't for John Rippey." Phil leaned forward with his elbows on his knees and took a last sip of his cocktail, then started into the tale.

"Ok so back in the eighties there was this raging house party at one of the big houses in the town site, Sven's place. You know the really nice house with the diesel generator. When you go in there now you can't even tell it's an off-the-grid house. Anyway, back then he only had a gas generator. So, he hosted this big party for all the hard cores up here, and they went full bore. I'm talkin' big sack of coke, bottles of whiskey, the whole nine. So this party starts raging, full tank of gas in the genny, all the lights are on, the music's blasting and people are getting FUCKED UP!" He looked around and his audience was captivated. "Then, later on, people start winding down, crashing on couches, passing out on the floor. Given the circumstances it really didn't seem too out of the ordinary. Until everyone is out, except Rippey, he's the last one awake, and he's camped out on a chair, eyelids sagging, and he watches as…Death comes through the door." At this point Phil was met with groans and fuck yous from the others, but he motioned for them to settle down.

Joneser, brimming with curiosity, asked, "What did it look like?"

"I don't know, as far as I know he never told anyone. He just says it was Death," Phil answered, then he continued.

"So Rippey see's this vision, or his idea of death, or something. Maybe it's not even a being, but just a sense of dread and he immediately knows what he has to do. He stands up and starts grabbing people one by one and drags them outside until he's pulled everyone out of the house. It turned out that the exhaust pipe on the generator that's supposed to funnel the fumes out of the basement, had vibrated loose, and it was displacing all the oxygen out of the house. If he had fallen asleep," Phil made a quick sweep of the circle, looking everyone in the eye, "they would all be dead."

Around the circle, arms prickled with goose bumps and everyone listening had eyes wide in disbelief. Many of them were thinking of the people he had saved, these were local pillars of the community, managers and co-workers at the lodge, regulars at the bar. To consider what it would be like if none of them had survived, was unimaginable.

Arliss was considering another aspect of the story and tried to verbalize his thoughts. "The idea that he saw a vision of a dark figure, or something kinda makes sense to me. It's as if his brain was just barely firing, you know, like it had started the shutdown procedure. And I bet that if all your life you believed that death comes with a 'white light,' then the last thing your brain shows you is a white light. In his case he believed death was something, maybe a figure, so the last thing his mind was prepared to show him was the dark figure he had always imagined."

"And you didn't see anything like that today, Sid?" Dan asked half-jokingly.

Sid smiled, "No man, mine happened so fast I just saw, snow, sky, snow, sky," and he made a rolling motion with one pointer finger. "Maybe I was never really that close to death, and I'm ok with that."

"Well, thanks for the ghost story Phil," Ray said as he stood up, "and the doobage, but I'm on breakfast shift tomorrow, so goodnight all." As he left, the gathering began to dissolve, and the guys decided they should head back to town. Plus they had to grab their stuff from the bar before it was locked up. They said goodnight to the rest of the lodge employees. Joneser offered Jenny a ride back to town. She accepted and went to gather her gear. Phil said he needed to go outside and shut off the big daytime generator and turn on the smaller nighttime unit. He said good-bye and walked out to the generator shed.

They walked quietly through the darkened main room of the lodge and reentered the bar. Thomas was starting to shut it down, so they filed through with the rest of the exiting patrons. Thomas began setting chairs upside down on the tables and spoke to the last three locals walking out, "Todd, ride safe. Jack, ride safe. Zeb, ride fast, take chances."

Zeb caught the slight as he was walking out the door, extended a middle finger and screeched, "Fuck you Tommy!" The Irwin locals revved up their sleds and tore off down the road in a pack, racing for the lead and howling into the darkness.

Jenny walked out in her snowboarding gear with a backpack and a helmet. She slid in tight behind Joneser and they roared off together. Sid tied both towlines to his sled and had even offered to carry Joneser's skis for him. Then he led the tired skiers back to the trailhead at a much slower pace. When they reached the trailhead and finally got to remove their ski boots they sighed with relief. Joneser was gone, his sled parked among all the others. He had gotten a ride into town in Jenny's car.

8.

The scare in the backcountry left Sid rattled for a few days. He started skiing more cautiously and picked up extra grooming shifts. This probably would have gone on indefinitely were it not for his friends. They taunted him relentlessly and mocked everything about the way he was skiing. Before long he couldn't take it anymore and was back to hucking big hits again, and shredding through the trees on the edge of control. The gang was satisfied that he was through his slump and things were getting back to routine. Johnny's snow making job had ended for the season and he had found a position selling outdoor gear at a local outfitter. Joneser and the lift mechanics mostly rode around on sleds and pretended to be busy. Cliff worked almost every night driving the bus around town and up to the mountain. He charmed the tourists and locals alike with his warm smile and friendly banter.

One of Cliffy's favorite pranks as a bus driver was to throw a flannel on over his uniform shirt and sit in a seat a few rows back while the bus loaded up with riders. Once everyone was on, and the other buses had left, his bus would be sitting still with no one in the driver's seat. Before long someone would yell from the back wondering about the driver, then others would always join in. This prank worked best if he had a few locals helping him out. Cliffy would yell out, "If he doesn't show up soon I'll drive this thing!" He would approach the driver's seat conspicuously watching for someone outside. Then, like a hijacker, he would jump into the seat, put it in drive and gun it out of the stop. Some riders would be shocked and speechless, while others cheered like revolutionaries. People always seemed to figure it out after he started hitting all the stops on time and, like all good pranks, it was fun while it lasted.

It was late morning, one day in February, when Cliffy woke up and joined the guys in the main room. They were moving slowly and putting together breakfast. Cliffy and Sid had both worked the previous night, while Joneser and Johnny had just stayed out late. Cliffy entered with a grin from ear to ear and just stood there with his hand behind his back, clearly hiding something. The guys looked up at him and he kept up his dumb grin and asked, "Guess what I have?"

Joneser, responded quickly, "Herpes!" Sid yelled "AIDS!," and lastly Johnny guessed, "Crotch Crickets!"

Cliffy rolled his eyes at these insults, "Please, I developed immunity to all of those by the time I was in the eighth grade. NO! You are wrong!" He whipped his hand in front of him and fanned out four white printed coupons. Who wants to ski Aspen tomorrow?"

"What?! No way?!" Sid pulled one out of Cliffy's hand and read it, "Holy shit! Where did you get these?"

Cliffy explained that during his shift he had held the bus at a hotel stop for a few minutes while two couples struggled to get their shit together. Once they were on, he recommended a good place for their dinner. Later, they found his bus again and said dinner had been great and they explained that they had booked four days at Aspen, but didn't like the snow so they had come to C.B, and they would not use the tickets, so they offered them to Cliff.

Cliff said, "I already traded my shift with Sarah."

Sid said, "Hell, I'm off."

Johnny said, "I'll call in sick." They all turned to Joneser while he averted his eyes and looked out the window.

"Man, I need to work, plus…I'm supposed to go out with Jenny tomorrow night."

Cliff and Johnny groaned in disappointment, but Sid smiled at him and gave the 'double guns' motion with both hands. "You dog, seems like you two are starting a little thing."

"Yeah, whatever," Joneser countered.

Johnny clapped Joneser on the shoulder and spoke down to him. "Look man, I am really pulling for you, but just remember, in C.B. you don't get the girl, you get your turn."

Joneser shrugged, "That's fine with me dude. I'm just trying to make it fun while it lasts." Then anger flared in his eyes, "Besides! It's fucking Aspen! I don't care if it's free, I hate that ski area. I hate that town and I especially hate that ski patrol! If I saw one of them on fire I wouldn't piss on him to put him out!"

"Whoa, dude calm down, what's your beef with Aspen?" Cliff asked, "It must be bad because I know how much you enjoy pissing on things, especially things on fire."

Johnny rolled his eyes and asked Cliff, "Seriously, you've never heard him bitch about Aspen?"

"I don't know, he bitches about so much, some of it just becomes white noise."

Sid smiled and eagerly sat down, "Oh, I love this story, it's so epically bad."

Joneser sat down and turned to Cliff, "So, I tried to live there before I came to C.B."

Cliff stifled a laugh, "Seriously? I have a hard time picturing you in a fur-lined one-piece."

"Fuck you, do you want to hear the story? My older brother had lived there a few years earlier and said how great it was. So, I got there in early fall, this was right after I graduated high school. I rented a place with four random douchebags and got a job washing dishes. It didn't pay shit, and didn't give you a pass, but I found another way to get a pass, I could be a ski packer."

Cliff interrupted," You mean, you would carry skis for rich people? I thought that was called a 'porter' or a 'sherpa'."

"God damn Cliffy, sometimes you are so dumb it hurts. No, for the first six weeks before the mountain opens, a group of ski packers, walks down all the steep runs with skis on and tries to get the snow to form a base, otherwise it might blow away into drifts. So every day eight of us would go out with this one ski patroller and we'd start at the top of a run and just step down a whole section, then he might make us hike back up and do another, or ride the lift back up if we were near one."

"I'm sorry," Cliff said, "but that sounds like the most ass-sucking job in the world."

"Yeah, dude, it did suck. Plus I was washing dishes at night. The only thing that made it tolerable was getting high. At first we were really sneaky, because we were supposed to be actual temporary ski area employees, and we had this really chill young ski patroller as our boss. He just made a joke of looking the other way every time we needed a safety meeting. So, after six grueling weeks of this shit, me and the seven other guys are stoked to finally be getting passes you know, like this shitty job is finally gonna pay off.

Then, POW! the day before our last day, the patroller we've had the whole time is nowhere around. They assigned us to like, the head patroller and his buddy. Those two worked us like dogs all morning, then they said all of us need to report to the med center at the base area and do a drug test. They say it's just a random drug screen. Of course none of us smoked that day, but it didn't matter, we all failed. Then they told us we had violated company policy and did not qualify for our ski passes."

"BURN!" Sid yelled out laughing, "Oh, man, that is such evil shit!"

"Yeah, so anyway, I had no pass and barely any money for rent. I tried to get a job with another department, like being a lifty, but I was black listed from the mountain. Plus, now the season had started and all the other jobs were gone. I hated my roommates, so I left Aspen in defeat. I pretty much stopped in C.B. just to check it out before I went home to Vermont, and I met Sid like an hour after I got to town."

"Ok," Cliffy said as he stood up, "that explains your smoldering hatred for Aspen. I'll remember that next time. I still don't understand your smoldering hatred for Daylight Savings, but I'm willing to let that one go."

"Who could not hate Daylight Savings?" Joneser asked rhetorically. "It makes absolutely no sense."

Joneser turned around to see if anyone was listening, and found that the other three had gone off to start packing their ski gear. He shook his head and muttered to himself.

The guys made a plan: they would leave early the next morning for the four-hour drive around the mountains dividing the two towns. Johnny declared he would buy a bag of weed before they left and he was heading over to see Crispy the local drug dealer. Sid joined him for the short bike ride a few blocks over.

They knocked on the door and Chris Peterson, aka 'Crispy,' greeted them with a warm smile and thin stony eyes. Crispy's enormous Rottweiler 'Honey Bear" pushed her wide black and brown head into Sid and demanded he scratch her neck before he even sat down. Her stumpy little sausage of a tail wagged frantically. Crispy was part owner of the best skate and snowboard shop in town and a well-known figure in the community, but his love of the herb prevented him from cutting free of his original profession as a pot dealer. He invited the guys to sit down in his cozy living room and loaded a bong that he passed to Sid, reloaded and then gave to Johnny. They chatted and got caught up. Sid asked, "Did Joneser ever tell you about the scale he stole for you?"

"No, really? He stole a scale, for me? He is such a good guy!"

"Yeah, but it didn't work out so well. It was a digital scale from the post office."

"Oohh?" Crispy rubbed the thin beard on his chin as he tried to picture the scenario. "Well I hope he didn't get in trouble on my account. He didn't get caught did he?"

"No," Sid said, starting to giggle, "He got it home, and we plugged it in, and it turns out it can only read in postage rates. Like, you'd put an eighth ounce on it and it would say $1.69." Crispy put his palm to his face and shook his head laughing. "You'd think there might still be a way to use that, if you could like, calculate the difference."

Johnny laughed also, "Yeah, I'd like to see that."

Honey Bear began an assault on Sid again, begging for affection. He tried to calm her down, but she was relentless. Crispy called to her to get down and pulled a golf ball from a drawer. "Here girl," he called and rolled it towards to kitchen as she bounded after it and happily lay down with it in her giant mouth.

"Oh! Dude!" Johnny exclaimed suddenly remembering the extra ticket. "What are you doing tomorrow? Want to ride Aspen with us for free?"

Crispy's eyes widened, "Oh, hell yeah! I was gonna work the shop, but I'll get someone to cover for me. Want me to drive?"

"No it's cool man, we can pile in the Galaxy," Sid told him.

"Aww, yeah, road trip in the hoopty." Crispy was genuinely stoked on this turn of events, "Hey, I've got some really good mushrooms if you guys are down for it! I'll give them to you for the ticket!"

"Wow, man, thanks, it might be good to get a little weird when we're over there. Maybe we'll run into Hunter Thompson," Sid said. Then the dog caught his attention. He watched in amazement as she opened her mouth wide and worked the golf ball back as far as it would go between her jaws. The muscles in her jaw tensed and she bit down hard, with a loud 'crack' the white shell of the ball split and brown strands of thin rubber band started spilling out. Crispy got to his feet and walked over to take the destroyed ball away before she ate it, saying with slight disappointment, "Oh, Honey, that one didn't even last ten minutes."

9.

It was still dark the next morning as the Galaxy sat idling outside the apartment. The tail pipe rumbled out a deep 'blub,blub,blub' and thin sheets of ice broke free from the top of the windshield and slid to the bottom like glaciers calving in the arctic. Three pairs of skis were already on the rack over the black vinyl top, so Crispy slid his snowboard into the gaping trunk on top of ski boots and gear bags with room to spare. Soon they were cruising past the old wooden sign that read 'Crested Butte, Elevation 8885.' The first hour went by quietly, Johnny had fallen back to sleep on the luxurious back seat. Cliffy rode shotgun and kept a running conversation with Crispy over the top of the front bench seat. Sid focused on driving and sipped coffee from an old Coleman thermos. The miles rolled by as the big studded snow tires hummed on the dry pavement.

By the time Johnny was rolling the third, or maybe fourth joint, the forest green sedan was pointed into the Roaring Fork river valley and before long they were pulling into a parking spot a block from the base lodge right after another car pulled out. Aspen Ski area doesn't have its own parking lot at the base area like most places. At the bottom of the mountain the town just starts. Most people park outside of town and ride a bus in. It was blind luck that Sid had found a spot on a side street near the base.

They slid into their ski gear and started walking toward the base area. From high up on the mountain three deep concussive booms echoed across the valley. It was the sound of ski patrol detonating bombs as they performed avalanche control.

The guys approached the ski area and noticed skiers walking away from the mountain, apparently already done skiing for the day.

"I bet this is a good place to clip tickets," Sid mentioned. Crispy agreed, "Yeah, that's crazy, people already leaving at ten o'clock. If they can't get first tracks they head home?" Clipping tickets was the technique of prowling the ski area parking lot and catching people as they left for the day. If you were a smooth talker and got lucky, you could convince someone to let you cut off their day ticket with a pair of wire snips. Then you could attach the ticket to your own jacket and ski for the remainder of the day. The process had roughly the same success rate as hitchhiking, but with much less chance of being murdered.

Luckily, begging for handouts was not on the schedule for today. Cliffy and Sid walked like kings to the ticket office to redeem the pre-purchased coupons for actual day tickets. There were a handful of skiers still purchasing tickets and the line moved quickly. When the guys got to the front they noticed handwritten signs on the ticket windows that read 'Cash only! No Credit or Debit, ATM in Base Lodge'.

They reached the window and found a bored girl about their age working the register. Cliff slid all four coupons through a semi-circle cut out in the Plexiglas window and Sid asked, "Why no credit card machines?" The girl responded like she had answered this question 1,000 times today, but seemed relieved it wasn't asked by an angry tourist.

"It's because of the World Cup Mogul Comp. Whenever we have a big event, like a competition, all the equipment they bring in for timing and communications messes with our phone lines and makes the credit card machines run super slow. Here are your tickets, have a good day."

She slid four tickets through the hole in the window. Cliffy picked them up and pulled four metal wire wickets from a little rack. Sid took a wicket and peeled the paper backing off of the lift ticket. He looped the wire through a D ring on his pants. Looking down as he walked, he tried to fold the adhesive side of the ticket onto itself. Still focusing on his ticket, Sid asked, "Have you ever seen one of those competition mogul runs?"

"Yeah I saw one at Vail one year," Cliff answered, "those things are scary, with huge kickers in the middle of each line, no thanks." They climbed the stone staircase leading out of the base area pavilion. At the top Cliff stopped briefly and turned back to look at the small ticket booth. Then he took a few quick steps to catch up with Sid as they walked towards the others waiting by the gondola terminal.

A short while later Crispy, Sid and Cliff stood on a cornice overlooking one of Aspen Mountain's famously steep double diamond runs. Johnny had hung back about fifty feet behind them.

"Clear?" Johnny asked his friends.

"You're good bro, stomp it." Crispy answered enthusiastically. Johnny took two hard skates to get going and aimed for the edge of the cornice. Just before his tips cleared the edge he twisted his arms and upper body to the left. His skis left the snow and took to the air as he unwound. Slowly he floated around in a full 360 as he continued to drop through the air. Having completed the spin, his skis touched down into the soft snow a shoulder width apart. The impact slammed Johnny's back to the snow, but he bounced up and immediately cut a hard turn and regained control.

With that opening move, the tone of the day was set. The others dropped the cornice and made big sweeping turns through soft wind pack snow at the top, changing into fluffy powder in the middle and ending with some chunky, harder stuff towards the bottom. Everyone was firing on all cylinders as they chewed up vertical feet. They attacked each run like bandits from the Wild West rolling into town, hooting and hollering. The group was jumping over anything they saw ahead of them and carving up the runs at full speed.

At a triple chair, they forced Cliffy into the singles line and he rode up with an older couple. The guys were waiting for him as he got off and could hear the couple still talking to him as they reached the top. They wished him good luck on *Rumspringa* and told him to make the decision that felt right in his heart. He told them he would, "With the Good Lord as his guide."

As he skated over to the guys, Crispy asked, "What the hell did you tell them?" "Yeah, what's *Rumspringa*?" Johnny demanded.

"Hey relax," Cliffy told them, "It's an Amish thing, you guys just wouldn't understand."

"So they were Amish?" Crispy asked, confused.

"No."

"So, you're Amish?"

"No," Cliffy said and then headed down the run, Crispy was left shaking his head in wonder. As Johnny slid past he said, "Yeah, try living with him."

Another time at the bottom of the triple chair, Sid got into the single line and ended up directly in front of the others in the maze. Sid was lined up with two strangers as the chair came around the bull wheel. Johnny and Cliff positioned the tips of their poles right over Sid's binding releases. Then as he lunged forward to get on the lift, they pushed down hard and clicked him out of his bindings. He fell flat on to the tips of his skis almost knocking over one of the other riders. The lifty hit the stop button and the lift ground to a halt as Sid's face grew bright red. He quickly set his skis straight and put them back on. His friends and some other skiers watching busted out laughing. Adding to the embarrassment, the lift op asked if he needed help getting on the lift. Crispy joined in saying, "You know sir, this lift doesn't service any easy runs, maybe you'd be more comfortable on Little Nell." At the top Sid had to admit it was a pretty clever move they had pulled, and he said the other people on the lift never spoke a word to him.

Around two o'clock they took a break for a late lunch. They wolfed down smashed peanut butter and honey sandwiches and Power Bars with the consistency of roofing shingles. Crispy pulled out a sandwich baggy filled with dried, long stemmed mushrooms. "You guys think it's time for these?"

Cliffy answered, "Honestly Chris, I don't think it's ever *not* time for those." They passed the bag around until it was empty and soon everyone was making disgusted faces as they chewed on the nasty fungus. They made one more run through the glades and decided maybe they should finish the day on groomers. This led to a giggling round of nonsense about 'shroomers on groomers. The level of skiing quickly devolved, and it started taking longer and longer to get down the runs. When the lifts closed, they carried their gear to the car. Standing next to the car, they changed out of ski gear and then piled in. The Galaxy easily slid into the exodus of slow moving ski traffic. Before long Aspen had vanished in the rear view mirror. In one of the small towns leading out of the valley they pulled into a fast food drive through and got some sodas and fries. With the psychedelics in full effect, no one had much of an appetite for anything more.

Crispy was in the co-pilot's seat for the ride home and he was taking his duty seriously. He rifled through the glovebox and found the perfect Jimi Hendrix tape. As " Hey Joe" spilled into the dark interior, Crispy paid close attention to the road, making sure Sid didn't get stuck in a lane that ended or miss any turns. Sid appreciated Crispy's effort, and it was comforting to have another set of eyes on the road. Sid generally considered himself very competent at operating under the influence of psychedelics, and tonight was no exception. As the fireworks went off behind his eyes, Sid felt that he was living 100% in the moment, hyper aware of his surroundings and confident enough to handle any situation. He applied the same philosophy to tripping that he used for hitting big jumps on the mountain. If you just sail off the jump passively, the lip can throw you off balance and leave you flailing. But if you come hauling into a big kicker eyes up, hands forward and pop hard with both feet right as you leave the ground, you are totally in control, plus you go even higher. You have to ride the trip, or it will ride you. This philosophy would be challenged as the red and blue lights of a police car came on directly behind the Galaxy. Sid gently eased the big car off the highway, slowed to a stop on a side road, and swallowed hard.

The crew calmy verified that all incriminating evidence was properly stowed. Then they waited, trying to appear perfectly innocent, as the officer approached the car. Sid cranked his window down and left the engine quietly rumbling. A bright flashlight beam came in through the rear window on the passenger side and swept over Johnny, moved to Crispy, then back to the driver's side where Cliff was scanned. Then the officer leaned his bushy mustache in through Sid's window, and asked, "May I see your license, registration and proof of insurance?" Sid motioned to Crispy to retrieve it from the glove box and Crispy swiftly handed the papers over. Sid added them to the license in his hand and gave them to the officer.

The cop briefly looked at the documents, and then stated, "I stopped you because one tail light is brighter than the other, and now I see that neither you nor your passengers are wearing seatbelts. I'm afraid that is a ticketable offense." This accusation hit Sid like a slap to the face because he wore his seatbelt religiously and knew Crispy had his on as well.

"Excuse me? We have seatbelts!" Sid exclaimed indignantly, as he grabbed the black plastic buckle of the lap belt and lightly shook it to show the cop.

"Oh, this vehicle only has lap belts?"

Sid said," Yeah, it's a '73." The policeman seemed to instantly dismiss the mistake, but Sid sensed himself approaching the lip of a jump and he was going to stomp this one big.

The policeman leaned in and looked Sid square in the eye. Sid's eyes were nothing but pupil as he stared up at the policeman. The policeman's tone changed very slightly and he asked, "Have you been drinking?" Sid noticed that the man was focused entirely on him. It was as if the other three in the car didn't even exist. Sid responded, "No, sir, we've just been skiing all day, now we are headed home."

"And you live in Crested Butte?"

"Yes, sir."

"Please step out of the car."

Sid had never done a roadside sobriety test, but he was in the frame of mind that this would be a fun challenge and chemically, he couldn't possibly fail it. It started out pretty basic, arms out, eyes closed, touch your nose, now on one foot. Then it rapidly became more advanced, as the officer demonstrated a pattern of touching his thumb to each finger on one hand and counting off, '1234,4321'. Sid flawlessly mimicked the action with his right hand as if he was qualifying for a speed trial. Then without being asked, he repeated the sequence on his left hand.

Frustration began to show around the walrus mustache and the officer's voice became even gruffer. He asked quickly, "Do you know your alphabet? I want you to say the alphabet starting with the letter 'H' and ending with the letter 'P". As fast as possible, Sid recited "HijklmnoP!" The officer was becoming disgusted with this whole exercise. He told Sid to stay still while he went to his car. Sid became mesmerized by the pulsing rhythm of blue and red lights. He turned

71

back to the Galaxy and flashed an illegal smile to the guys inside. The policeman returned and began to assemble a breathalyzer unit. He asked for Sid's consent and then explained what Sid had to do. Sid then blew into the straw as hard as he could. The officer read the results, then assembled another unit and had him repeat the test. When the results again showed a BAC of 0.000, the officer had to admit defeat. He ushered Sid back to the Galaxy, then quickly wrote out a warning to fix the one dim taillight.

Sid thanked him, slid the shift lever into D and pulled away. They had to turn around and drive past the parked police cruiser, but once they pulled back onto the highway the car exploded with cheers and laughter. Sid's leg was shaking so hard, it was making the accelerator pulsate. No one could believe how close they had come to going to jail. With that obstacle behind them they made the rest of the trip feeling like conquering heroes returning to the homeland.

10.

Across the country, in the small town of Canaan, CT about twenty-five employees at Becton Dickinson Corporation were gathered in the breakroom to celebrate the retirement of one of their most senior technicians. A man named John Rippey had worked 33 years with the company using advanced injection-molding processes to create sterile plastic syringes and a myriad of other products for the medical field. As the Branch Manager handed him a piece of cake, John announced he would be filing for Social Security the very next day. He smiled at old friends and explained how he hoped to travel the country visiting his children and grandchildren. All his coworkers shook his hand and wished him well.

11.

The winter had peaked and closing day for the ski area loomed closer on the calendar. Each of the guys in apartment 203 had skied at least a few days every week, and the effort was starting to take its toll. Cliff had managed to jam his thumb skiing bumps and could barely hold a pen to write. Johnny was walking with a slight limp after tweaking his 'good' knee. And Sid had gone sledding up to the lodge with some other riders one wicked cold night. He recieved frostbite in the gap between his goggles and the lower face guard of his helmet. Now, whenever it got even a little bit cold two pink shapes that looked like NIKE 'Swooshes' appeared under his eyes. Joneser was the lone survivor physically, but his blossoming romance with Jenny the Smurf had gone down in flames.

Cracks in the relationship first started to show one night at a house party. He had returned from the bathroom to see her leaning in to her ex-boyfriend kissing him while he sat in a chair. She noticed Joneser and pushed herself away from the ex and made a big scene. She told Joneser she had just leaned in to say hi, when the ex grabbed her and kissed her. "Sure, whatever," Joneser said and he let the incident slide. Then only a few days later the whole crew had gone out to hear a ska band play at a bar downtown. The Coronado bar has an open second story deck in the front overlooking the street. The show ended and everyone filed out into the street, but Jenny said she needed to get something and went back in. The guys were waiting for her outside. Looking up, they saw her return to the upstairs deck and find that same guy. She sloppily made out with him again, oblivious to the fact that she could easily be seen from below.

The guys were pretty shocked, but they didn't say much about it as they turned and walked back to the Whispering Pines. The next day she found Joneser and demanded to know why he had rudely abandoned her at the bar. Joneser told her what he had seen and she adamantly denied it, but he was done. He had had his turn.

With that in mind, Sid felt Joneser needed an adventure. He heard about a sled trip to Aspen some other guys were planning, so he got them in. Despite his dislike for the ski area, Joneser had to admit that the adventure sounded pretty epic. They would leave from C.B. South early, ride through Cement Creek along Reno Road and onto Taylor Pass, cross over the high alpine pass and end up at The Sundeck on the top of Aspen Mountain.

It was a beautiful spring morning when they unloaded the sleds from a trailer behind Joneser's black and rust Chevy pick up. Two other guys were already there and the last rider arrived minutes later. Sid only knew John McCabe, another snow groomer from the ski area, but he and Joneser were introduced to his friend Caleb, and another rider named Josh Mazer. McCabe's Skidoo was nearly identical to Sid's, but the other two machines were fairly uncommon for this area.

With a slight build and short blond hair, Josh straddled a white 440 XCR Polaris race sled. The light, nimble machine had a short

136-inch track with paddles and a powerfully modified 440cc engine. Whenever Josh removed his helmet, he lit a cigarette in almost the same motion and had the air of an experienced snocross racer fully confident in his machine.

Caleb was funny and likeable, and he was a big boy. Built like a wrestler, Caleb's machine reflected his size. It was a massive, green and black Arctic Cat 'Thundercat' with a 900cc motor. The sled looked like it would be more suited for racing across lakes in Minnesota than climbing mountains in Colorado. But Caleb's sled appeared to be in great shape, and ready to rip.

Red plastic gas cans hung from all five sleds, with each rider coming up with their own design for securing them. Some were slung with one on each side like saddlebags. Others were bungee corded or ratchet-strapped to the rear bumpers.

A quick check determined everyone had avalanche gear and the sleds' oil bottles were full. With that, Josh flicked away his cigarette, pinned the throttle and they all followed him out the trail. The first section was down a fast tree lined road that rolled gently over small hills. They only slowed to secure gas cans, and made good time.

Forty minutes in, they had completed the first leg of the journey and come out of the trees into a wide-open valley looking out across Taylor Park Reservoir. The ice had already started to recede from the edges of the big lake, and open water rippled gently in the light breeze. After a long section of whoops, the trail smoothed out as it entered the Taylor Park Valley. Here they stopped and topped up the fuel tanks and ate a few snacks. McCabe the group leader, explained that this would be a pretty fast section and hard to see through the roost of the sled ahead of you. He told them to leave some space and avoid rear-ending anybody. He would signal for the turn well ahead of the cut off. They found a tree well that looked inconspicuous and placed the jugs of remaining fuel into it, then shoveled snow on to cover them up.

With a quick tug of the starter rope each sled fired back up, each sled except the Arctic Cat. Caleb's big arm desperately yanked on the cord but the Cat would not even sputter. His arm was obviously getting tired and Sid offered to give it a pull if he would hold the throttle wide open. The strong smell of gas indicated it was already flooded. Sid grabbed the plastic handle and expected it to pull over similarly to his 500. He jerked the cord and was stunned when the resistance felt as heavy as pulling a cinder block. "Thump, thump, thump." The engine slowly made a full rotation. "Holy shit dude!" Sid exclaimed.

"Yeah, it's kind of a bear," Caleb admitted with mild embarrassment. Josh jumped off his sled and walked over to Sid. "I'll get this bitch going," he said with confidence. Sid and Josh managed to each get a hand on the handle and Caleb squeezed the throttle. After the first pull they became synchronized and started spinning the motor faster and faster. Before long it coughed and farted, then roared to life in a cloud of smoke. Caleb smiled and thanked them. Soon all five sleds were flying along the trail again. Without the awkward extra fuel tanks each rider could crouch over bumps and throw the sled around with better agility.

They entered an area that was covered in tracks. Riders could approach from Leadville or Buena Vista to reach this high alpine playground. Groups of other riders could be seen high marking big faces or jumping off windlips, but despite how fun that looked, the team stuck to their mission. They knew that every drop of fuel would be needed to reach their goal and return.

Once they were through the playground they started climbing. Higher and higher they went until there were no longer any trees in sight. A cold wind blew across the top of the ridge despite the bright sunny day. The wind had erased tracks even a few hours old and piled drifts over the trail. Thick wooden posts spaced every few hundred feet stuck out of the snow indicating the course of the trail. In some cases the posts stuck out about three or four feet, while other times they might just see six inches of a post. There was still a lot of snow at this elevation. It was breathtaking to ride along the highest ridges of the mountains. Aside from the trail markers, they couldn't see signs of civilization in any direction. The trail led to a long steep decent bridging the gap between two peaks. One by one they dropped down the ridge, picking up speed.

Once they all reached the level area at the bottom Sid looked back at the steep wall they had come down and briefly considered what it would be like to climb it on the way home. But Josh's little white XCR quickly reminded Sid of the task at hand as it screamed up the next ridge bringing them closer to Aspen Mountain.

Gradually they began dropping out of the higher elevation and back down to the timberline. They joined up with a more heavily traveled trail and started seeing other sleds again. McCabe flagged down a pair of riders going the opposite way and briefly asked them about the best way to the Sundeck. They shouted some directions to him over the idling engines and pointed down the trail. Again, the crew started moving, climbing up through a section of trees and coming to a line of orange plastic fencing. Signs indicated this was the ski area boundary and snowmobiles were strictly prohibited. The five C.B. riders shut down their machines and took off their helmets. They crossed the boundary and walked up the hill a short way. Through the trees they started to hear the music of the Grateful Dead. As they got closer they saw a magnificent gray wooden building with a stone chimney and a huge wooden deck.

A lunchtime crowd of skiers filled lounge chairs and picnic tables outside. The guys secured a table and sat down. Josh lit a fresh cigarette and blew the smoke out the side of his mouth. Caleb and McCabe each went to get a beer from the overpriced cafeteria. Sid and Joneser pulled food and water from their backpacks and swapped sledding tales with Josh.

Joneser was munching a handful of bright orange corn chips. He absently held one up as he said something about new shocks he wanted for his sled. In the brief moment he looked away from the chip, a Gray Jay landed on the deck railing and snatched the chip from his fingers. Just as quickly the bird flew off into the trees with the chip in its beak. "God damn!" Sid exclaimed, "The camp robbers around here are bold!"

Josh chuckled, "Yeah man, it's the law of the wild. If you want something you just gotta go for it!"

Joneser muttered something about killing the bird and pulled his baggie of chips in closer. Sid swallowed a bite of apple and opened his mouth to say something else when someone loudly called out to them, "Slide over bitches!" McCabe and Caleb came back to the table, each holding a frosty pint glass of amber brew. Josh made a point to scoot over and declared, "Whoa, make way for the rich folk. How much were those?"

McCabe retorted, "You really don't want to know," then he took a big sip, savored it and said, "Mmmmm, but oh, so worth it!"

Caleb smiled. "I had to finance this beer. Three more payments and this baby's mine!" The guys chuckled and took in the scene. Forearms and backs had started to ache from the long ride, and they still had to make it back.

"So how many times have you done this ride?" Joneser asked McCabe.

"This is the second time I've made it, but I've tried three times. And so far," he rapped his knuckles on the table twice, "this has been the smoothest. The first time I went with Rippey and some other guys. The snow covered most of the posts at that top section, so they were just going off memory. We made a couple wrong turns, but we got here eventually." He took another sip, "You don't notice it if you stay on the trail, but there are cliffs and cornices right off of either side. I think going later in the season like this really helps."

"How did the other time go?" Sid asked him.

"Well, that time I was leading, and we were blowing down that really fast straight coming off of Taylor. All of the sudden I see the turn right ahead, so I grabbbed a handful of brake. Then I hear a noise and see a sled go tumbling past me! I didn't know my friend Rob was so close behind me, and of course he couldn't see through my roost. When I slowed way down, he swerved to avoid my ass and lost control. He was pretty banged up. And he tore something in his shoulder. So we headed back. I really felt bad. So, that's why I wanted you guys to stay off each other's asses down there."

The crew finished lunch and refilled water bottles. They talked to a few local skiers who were impressed by their journey. Encouraged, they packed up and walked back to the sleds. Each of them checked their fuel level and oil tanks. Josh said he had a siphon hose if they ended up needing to transfer fuel. Sid had two quarts of injection oil in the rear compartment of his seat and added some to his sled, since oil was just as vital as fuel.

The Thundercat started fairly easily, giving them hope that it would be a smooth ride home. Thirty minutes later, those hopes were dashed as they reached the long climb they had previously come down. Caleb's big Cat gunned it to the hill as fast as possible. He made it about halfway up then lost power and started to slow. Caleb turned it around and came back to the bottom where the others were waiting and watching. Caleb had a go it it again with the exact same results. After the second time, Josh said, "Let me try!" and he switched places with Caleb. This took fifty or sixty pounds off the machine. Josh rode the sled out and got a running start. With his feet in the stirrups he crouched over the seat and punched the throttle. Up he climbed, past the halfway, then the tone of the exhaust changed and the engine bogged down, a hundred feet from the top he turned back and returned to the others.

"Damn!" said Josh, "This thing does not like altitude."

"Yeah," agreed McCabe, "This is not good, do you know what jets are in it?" he asked Caleb.

"Ah, no," was the response

Josh took command of the situation and ran down some basic checks on the sled, With a Leatherman pocket tool, he removed the air box and verified all three carburetor slides would fully open. Next he pulled the spark plugs to see if any were fouled. He installed three new plugs and checked the fuel lines for pinches or kinks, then he reassembled the machine and started it up, it sounded a little better with new plugs. Josh took another run at the hill, again the machine faltered two thirds of the way up and returned to the bottom, daunted.

McCabe looked concerned. "Guys we need to get going or we'll be riding back in the dark."

"Can we tow it?" Joneser offered. He was reclined on his saddle with his head resting on the handle bar pad. "I've got a ten foot strap."

Josh nodded at the idea and Caleb enthusiastically encouraged them, "Yeah, let's try that!" Caleb liked any idea right now that didn't involve leaving his sled for dead out in the wilderness.

They decided Joneser would pull the Cat with Josh riding it, and Caleb would ride the XCR up. They hooked up the sleds and hit it. The Polaris growled and dug into the steep hillside with its paddles digging for traction. Josh expertly positioned the Cat and feathered the throttle enough to help climb, but not so much that he rear ended Joneser. Snow streamed off Joneser's track and pounded the hood and windshield of the Cat as Josh ducked down and tried to dodge the roost. In this manner they peaked the ridge and came out on top triumphantly. The others quickly joined them and gave high fives all around. Caleb graciously thanked Joneser who patted the hood of his trusty steed. Josh unhooked the sleds while Caleb cleaned the snow off his hood. They all got going again and ran hard the next ten miles, stopping only to make sure everyone was keeping up.

There were no other sleds in the Taylor Park play area as they passed by this time, but everyone was feeling more confident they could beat the setting sun. The sleds hammered along the bumpy trail on the side of the reservoir and made it to the fuel cache. Each sled was close to a quarter tank when they emptied what was still left in the jugs from earlier. Caleb swung his empty jug onto his seat and heard something 'thunk' inside it. He shook the jug side-to-side and confirmed something was definitely inside the jug. He opened the cap and pulled out the flexible nozzle. He then looked in. The first thing he saw were strands of fine gray hair swirling in the remaining drops of gasoline. Then he shook the jug to the side and found the limp remains of a decomposing mouse. The smell of death blended with the vapor of high octane. "UUGHHH, nasty!" he cried as he wrinkled his nose.

He told the others what he'd found, and Josh smiled with understanding."Well, there 'ya go! You have mouse hair restricting your fuel filter, maybe even your suction tube!"

Caleb looked at the dead mouse again muttering, "You little shit."

The remainder of the trip didn't require any big climbs, only long sections of punishing whoops. But all the sleds made it safely to the trailhead. It had been an exciting adventure for everyone, and they had accomplished their goal: they had made it to Aspen and back in a day.

12.

Closing day for the ski area was a massive celebration. Joneser and the other lift mechanics were on the clock, but for the most part they just rode around on sleds visiting people. Cliff also had to work, but the busses were like rolling parties, ferrying locals and tourists alike up to the base area for free concerts, drink specials and end of the season mayhem. Johnny skied hard through the morning, then ran into friends at the upper warming hut and started drinking gin and tonics in the sun. Sid was skiing the front side making laps through the singles line when he met up with two girls on vacation with their families. He spent the rest of the day acting as their guide, showing them fun lines across the mountain.

When the lifts shut down he and the girls were gliding past the Silver Queen chair when he heard his name being called. Sid looked up and saw Joneser and several other lift mechanics hanging out above the bullwheel platform over the lift terminal. He ushered the girls into the terminal and up a metal ladder into the service access, then they came out overlooking the crowds of partiers gathered at the base of the mountain.

C.B. Mountain was famous for the naked skiers on the last day of the season and they were due to arrive any minute. Typically the naked skiers were folks who started drinking earlier in the day, and by five o'clock, when the parade began, they were pretty sloppy. The logistics of the feat took a little planning, because they had gone up the hill with clothes, but now had to come down without. Some riders stuffed their clothing into backpacks, or handed them to a trusted friend who would hopefully meet them at the bottom. Many snowboarders just opted to drop their pants around their ankles and ride down that way. Once naked, they still had to demonstrate enough skill to make it down a steep blue run to the bottom. This challenge was too difficult for many of the drunkest. The crowd of spectators collectively cringed and groaned at naked buttcheeks and boobs covered in big swathes of bleeding roadrash from sliding down an icy slope.

Sid and the crew on the bullwheel cheered with delight as each pale, shriveled and possibly bleeding body came down the hill. He had to wonder if some of them even knew how to ski as they spent more time on their freezing asses than standing. A huge cheer roared from the crowd as a group of more skilled skiers started launching off a small jump on the side of the run. Sid made a double take and realized that the skier wearing only a long red and white knitted beanie with a huge pompom on top was his own roommate Johnny. Johnny blasted off the jump and threw a huge spread eagle, with arms and legs fully extended. He touched down and squeezed his legs together as he swished down the hill in classic ski form.

Eventually the last skier came off the mountain and the ski season was officially over. The crew climbed down from the lift and Sid introduced the girls to Joneser and asked if they would like to get some dinner together. The girls declined, saying they had plans, then said goodbye and headed to their hotel. Sid admitted that it was still fun trying. He and Joneser spotted a table full of friends and spent the evening getting shitfaced while listening to live music from an outside stage.

13.

At the office of the Social Security Administration in Torrington, Connecticut, an SSA worker was processing the file for John Rippey of Canaan, Connecticut when she noticed a flaw. All his paperwork appeared in order: his birth certificate put him at 65 years of age, his SS# matched his birth certificate, and he had filed income tax in this state for the last 43 years…But why did he have several years of income tax filing at the Denver branch of the SSA also? She ran a quick check. Often times military or contract workers file income outside of their state of residency, but both the Colorado filings and the Connecticut filings were listed as the sole state of residency, and each was for complete year periods. No partial year status indicated he had moved locations in the middle of a year. She rubbed the bridge of her nose with her thumb and forefinger. In a country where everyone tries to pay as little taxes as possible, why was this guy paying twice what he had too? She printed both files and walked to her supervisor's office.

14.

Over the next week, the town transitioned into the biannual ski town condition of 'Mud Season'. In the spring this happens when the mountain has closed, but the mountain bike trails are too muddy to be ridden, the snowmelt has not filled the rivers for paddling and none of the summer tourists have started arriving yet. A similar event takes place in the fall, when all the joys of summer have passed, but the snow hasn't started falling yet. Over the course of a month the town population is decimated. All of the seasonal jobs end, owners of some local business's close up temporarily and go to Hawaii or Central America and many people just move on to a new place.

For the guys of apartment 203, the first week of May is a week of scavenging and salvage. Tenants hastily move out of apartments and rental houses on the last day of the month and are forced to take only what will fit in a UHaul, sometimes even as little as what fits into the back of a Subaru wagon. This means that the dumpsters in the alley might contain such treasures as skis with one broken binding, a mountain bike missing a wheel, stereos, TVs you name it. And some years it's not even limited to small stuff. Big scores in the past had seen beater cars and snowmobiles left behind for one reason or another

The guys walked down an alley passing a joint back and forth. Cliff walked with a pair of ski poles he had found and Sid carried a coffee maker that looked to be in good condition. They rounded the corner and Johnny's eyes widened, "YESSS!" he called out. He ran towards a snowmobile pushed along side a big dumpster, a late afternoon sunbeam shined on the glossy fiberglass hood. The others walked up, noticing drag marks in the dirt alley that trailed from the metal skis of the sled to a nearby garage.

"Oh, man," Sid spoke as he contemplated the potential of the machine. It was a Yamaha from the early eighties with duct tape patching the seat together and multiple cracks across the hood, he also noticed it was missing the handle from the pull start. Sid set down the coffee maker and opened the hood. Nothing else really mattered if it failed the first test. He gripped the drive clutch firmly and tried to get the motor to turn over. It would not move one millimeter. The engine was totally seized. "Aww, sorry man," he looked up at Johnny with sympathy. "Maybe we'll find another one with a good motor."

They continued on, Joneser spied some skis sticking out of a garbage can. He decided to leave them when he saw that six inches of one edge was completely torn off. They were about to turn back when Cliffy noticed something. "Oh, no way, did Hippy Dan abandon his bus?" They all looked, and there in an empty lot behind some industrial buildings sat a full sized yellow school bus with neat black letters down the side reading Mesa County Public School District.

"Let's check it out," Joneser said with growing excitement as they walked across the lot towards the bus. "That guy was a dick."

"I don't think I knew Hippy Dan." Sid said.

"Oh, you've seen him: short little white guy with dreads. He was always hanging out at the Coronado."

"Ok, yeah that guy. He seemed a lot like a trustifarian to me."

"Oh, totally," Cliffy picked up the back-story. "He was the kind of trusty where his parents just agreed to keep sending checks as long as he never came home. He came to town and tried to start a glass shop. That's what this building is, well, was. It's empty now." Cliff pointed a ski pole at a gray unremarkable commercial building in front of the bus.

Johnny stepped to the bus and easily slid open the folding glass door. The guys all climbed up the stairs and stood inside. All the rows of passenger seats had been removed. On the floor sat a few unopened boxes of laminate wood flooring, but the rest of the bus sat empty. "Hey, Cliffy," Joneser asked, "is this your first time on a school bus this long?"

Johnny laughed and started walking to the rear of the bus, "So he was going to convert this into a camper I take it?" Sid asked.

"Yeah, he wanted to build this camper and go on Rainbow Family Tour with his girlfriend," Joneser answered. "Then the glass shop went under, and the two of them went to Burning Man. The girlfriend never came back. Shortly after that, Hippy Dan just eased on down the road."

"How do you guys know all about this dude?" Sid asked.

Cliffy answered, "You know that guy Slade who lives downstairs? He's an actual glass blower, and he tried to work with Dan in his shop. But he said it was a total shit show. Like, Dan had no idea how to do *anything*. He just had money to open a glass shop. Then he thought he could get high and just have Slade do all the work."

"This would make a pretty sick shuttle vehicle," Johnny called out from the middle of the bus. "Or we could park it way out in the woods as a secret back country cabin!"

"I like that idea!" Sid said pointing at Johnny, "I'm going to check out the engine." Sid walked outside and undid the rubber straps on either side of the big fiberglass hood. He put his foot on the bumper and tipped the whole nose of the bus forward. Beneath the hood sat a big V8 engine. Sid made a quick inspection, checking vital fluids and looking for any signs of catastrophic failure. All in all it looked to be in pretty good shape.

Johnny was sitting in the drivers seat running his fingers along the visor overhead and then under the seat and any other place that keys might be hidden. He slid the driver's window open and said to Sid, "No keys anywhere."

"Bah, that's not a big deal." Sid said as he tipped the hood back into place. "I bet the batteries are shot though." Sid walked around to the driver's side and opened a metal panel on the side of the bus. Inside sat two massive truck batteries. Sid leaned in and confirmed that instead of having nice flat sides, each of the batteries looked bulging and swollen.

Johnny was still leaning out the window and Sid looked up at him and said, "yeah these are no good, they've been frozen solid."

They left the bus and started walking back, Cliffy and Joneser tried to see how far they could walk with their eyes closed, each using a ski pole as a blind man's cane. Then Joneser whacked Cliffy hard across the back of his calf with the pole and Cliffy threw his pole at Joneser like a javelin.

So it went for the month of May. Joneser's job was year round, but his hours were cut to part time and the days he worked he spent doing menial jobs like reupholstering the chair lift cushions. Cliff still had two weeks off until the busses started running again on the summer schedule. Sid and Johnny were officially unemployed and trying to make their meager savings last. They didn't go to bars and they didn't go out to eat. The Galaxy sat parked with only a quarter tank of gas. Life just slowed down, and nobody really seemed to mind.

The mud season gave them a chance to get their mountain bikes out of storage in a friend's garage and perform some preseason maintenance and repairs. The bikes had been put away dirty and broken in the fall, and it had been easy to ignore how much work they needed to be rideable again. Sid and Johnny were the most capable bike mechanics, so they set up shop one day on the dilapidated wooden picnic tables outside on the rotting deck of the apartment building. They had tools and rags spread out and organized as they went through each bike.

The day before, the guys had searched through the couch cushions, under the floor mats of the car and in backpacks and coats to find enough money to buy some alcohol. What they decided on was a large plastic bottle of bottom-shelf Gordon's vodka. They mixed this with red Kool-Aid for a tasty, low budget, cocktail. Sid and Johnny each had a tall glass of bright red goodness with them as they labored. Sid worked to straighten a rear wheel that had been knocked severely out of true. His precision technique involved beating the rim against the table for the initial adjustment, then loosening several spokes on one side of the wheel and tensioning the opposite spokes until they were tighter than banjo strings. This allowed the rim to roll between the brake pads while only rubbing hard in a few spots.

Johnny was sorting through a small pile of used brake pads that had previously been taken off the bikes. He was looking for pads that were in better shape than the ones currently installed. Cliffy came home around noon and joined them on the deck. He pulled out a Ziploc baggie of freshly purchased weed and started to pack a bowl.

"Nice Cliffy. Way to manage your finances," Johnny said acting impressed.

"Like I always say," Cliffy responded, "weed gets you through times with no money better than money gets you through times with no weed!"

Johnny laughed at him, "You're gonna need to be high to ride on these worn out brakes."

Cliffy shot back, "I feel like those things just slow me down anyway. Who needs 'em?" He took a big pull from his pipe, and then started coughing uncontrollably. Johnny and Sid both stopped working to watch him as he dramatically held his chest and tried to regain his composure. With eyes watering, he finally drew in a full breath and let out a long, "Wheeeeoowww!"

"Damn, dude. You sure Crispy didn't sell you a bag of drier lint and lawn clippings?" Sid asked. Cliffy finished the bowl with another big hit, then blew out a huge puff of smoke, this time without a single cough. "Would you like one?" Cliffy asked Sid.

"I'd love that."

"Excellent," Cliffy said while he loaded the bowl, "And which would you prefer, stems or seeds?"

That night, they were all home, and had all four bikes leaned against the wall in the apartment. Joneser had showered and was brushing knots and tangles out of his long hair. He kept looking at his bike, amazed at the work that had been accomplished. "So, seriously? I have all three rings working again? That's awesome!" Joneser had finished the season last year with a broken front shift cable. He had adjusted the stops so the chain stayed locked in the middle ring. This was less than ideal, but he had managed some long rides like this.

"You can shift to the big ring," Johnny explained, "but that big ring isn't great. You have five teeth completely folded over. I tried to fold one back and it just snapped off, so I rotated the ring on the crank, now when you bottom out on a rock you can start wrecking other teeth."

"Thanks dude, I think this is gonna be an epic season," Joneser predicted.

A week later, Sid was getting a few groceries at the local market, and as he waited in the checkout line he scanned the cover of the latest POWDER magazine. On it was C.B's local ski hero Seth Morrison carving a big mountain turn in Alaska. Sid continued waiting in line, when he noticed that two people ahead of him, with bright pink dyed hair, stood Seth Morrison himself! Sid's mind was blown as he watched one of the best skiers in the world walk past the bulletin board and out the door carrying two bags of groceries. Seeing the board reminded Sid that he needed to find a job. The ski area had not offered any summer time work this year.

Sid stood in front of the corkboard covered with thumbtacked fliers for upcoming bands, roommates wanted and yes! a few jobs. He quickly glanced over the handwritten notices: dishwasher, *no*, river rafting guide, *maybe*, equipment operator/laborer, *yes*!

He hung his grocery bag over the handlebar of his townie and headed straight to the address. He knew it was the right place by the various pieces of heavy equipment parked on the dirt street. A concrete building sat on the corner with a small sign that read Joe's Backhoe. A large bay door big enough for equipment to drive through was open, but in the bright afternoon sunshine the interior looked like a dark cave. Sid parked his bike and walked to the doorway. His eyes tried to adjust to the darkness as he called out, "Hello?"

"Come on in," he heard. He entered the shop and found a big blue Mack dump truck filling one half of the room with shovels, rakes and other smaller tools leaning against the wall. He walked around the truck and found a break area with five men sitting on plastic chairs around a small table covered with motorcycle magazines. "What can I do for you?" asked Joe Green the owner. He had brown hair streaked with gray and a long mustache.

"Are you still hiring?" Sid asked.

"Hey, I know him," someone called out whom Sid hadn't noticed because he was bent over leaning into a small fridge. Sid looked at him and realized it was John Rippey, his savior. Sid smiled at John, then reached his hand out to Joe and introduced himself. "Well, what can you do?" asked Joe. Sid was a little embarrassed, he hadn't expected an interview in front of the entire crew. But he had walked right in without calling or submitting an application, so he kind of asked for it.

"Well Joe, I'm a cat operator for the mountain, but I've run backhoes and skidsteers before. I know how to move dirt."

"Ok, that's good." Joe looked at him and considered, "Can you run a number two round point hand excavator?" Sid paused for a moment trying to figure out which type of equipment that could be, then he realized that it was simply a basic shovel.

He smiled wide and answered, "Oh I'm a black belt with one of those." This got some chuckles from the crew.

Joe turned to Rippey, "So you know this kid?"

"Yeah, we had a bit of an adventure last winter. I can say his skiing style is unlike anything I've ever seen." Rippey winked at Sid.

"Alright then, that's a good enough reference for me," Joe said. "Do you have a driver's license?" Sid nodded, "OK, be here Monday at seven, with workboots and your lunch. We'll see how the day goes, and then we can talk about pay. Sound good?"

Sid was stunned by how easy that had been, he stammered, "Yuh, yeah. That sounds great. Thanks a lot Joe." He looked at Rippey, "Thanks Rippey!" Then he turned and walked out without even meeting the other workers. He figured he would meet them come Monday.

15.

Sid loved the new job. He would ride his cruiser to the shop early every morning. The whole crew would gather and drink coffee while they worked out the days plan. Then they would break into smaller teams and head to different job sites scattered all over town.

88

To Sid's delight he always ended up working with Rippey. For the first few weeks the two of them worked exclusively clearing pads for a row of new homes with Atlas the Bulldozer.

When Sid first saw Atlas he was stupefied. The massive D8 Caterpillar was sparkling in the morning sunlight. He had seen big machines before, but none that sparkled like this. As they parked the pickup next to it he noticed artwork lining the edges of the blade and running down the side of the machine. Even most of the undercarriage had been covered in intricate patterns of hardfacing.

Hardfacing is a form of welding that lays extremely hard material over the base metal to protect it from wear. It can often be seen as a series of lines or dots on the cutting edges of buckets and blades. But Atlas was so much more than that. For one thing, the design was not simple lines or dots. It was beautiful flowing characters that each joined together like cursive writing. In places it looked like Egyptian hieroglyphics and in other spots it looked like Elvish runes from the Tolkien books. The hardface would not rust, and it reflected a shiny, almost chrome-like surface glimmering in contrast to the faded CAT yellow paint that covered the rest of the machine.

Up by the operator's seat, black and white letters in a bold font read ATLAS. This was probably the name of a previous owner's company as it was obvious the dozer had been around for decades. Sid assumed it had to be from the sixties at least, because it didn't have the big roll cage frame that all modern machines have. And when Rippey started cranking on a small gas powered 'pony motor' connected to the big diesel engine, Sid knew he was looking at an authentic piece of history.

Rippey explained that he had run the dozer for Joe every summer for years. It had already been hardfaced when he first saw it. Joe explained that a welder they called 'The Swede' ate some mushrooms once and stayed up all night with a full box of hardfacing rod. In the morning they found Atlas transformed into a piece of rolling artwork.

A special machine needed a special operator, and Rippey seemed to be the one. He had developed a feel for how deep the blade was cutting just from the sound of the load on the engine and the vibration of the tracks.

Sid was trained to be Rippey's guide. He would stand on the ground and hold the grade rod. This calibrated measuring stick would take a reading from the laser transit and tell Sid how much dirt they needed to remove to reach the correct grade.

After a few mistakes early on, Sid learned that adding dirt back to the pad and then compacting it with a 'jumping jack' was a big waste of time. He needed to pay closer attention and not remove too much dirt. But, it also wasted time to make lots of little cuts only removing an inch at a time. Soon Sid figured out how to read each cut more accurately and give Rippey just the right hand signal for his next pass. Rippey learned to interpret Sid's hand signals and adjust the blade as it sliced into the soil. Each site preparation went quicker than the last and Joe was very pleased with the progress.

When they shut down Atlas at the end of each day, the two of them went over the machine from top to iron-plated bottom. They greased all the fittings and checked the fluid levels. Often they had to tighten up track plates that had come loose or make other adjustments. While they worked, the pair kept a running conversation. Rippey spoke about town politics in the small community and how Crested Butte had changed over the years. Or he told amazing stories from his days on the snowmobile racing circuit and life in C.B in the eighties. Each story contained some hidden wisdom or Rippey's clever sense of humor.

Most days after work, Sid still had time to sneak in a mountain bike ride with the guys before it got dark, or at least before it got *really* dark. Johnny and Cliff had both started working again and summer was in full swing. Families of tourists crowded down town, and new people cycled in replacing those that had left. The days were warm and sunny, but evenings still required a sweatshirt and hat.

One warm day, Sid and Cliffy were flirting with two girls who worked for the town landscape maintenance department. The girls were in charge of all the decorative flower boxes located throughout the town, but today they were busy hanging banners from all the light posts in preparation for the upcoming One World Music Festival on Labor Day weekend. Cliffy was working his charm, helping one girl unfold banners while Sid held the ladder for the other girl standing on it. She reached up and her t-shirt pulled up over her shorts, exposing her midriff. Sid definitely did not notice as the bland government sedan pulled behind him and parked at the police station. If a horn-helmeted Viking had gotten out of the car, he wouldn't have noticed that either. Instead an average looking, middle-aged man in a shirt and tie got out and walked into the police station. He explained he was an inspector with the Social Security Administration.

The next day, Rippey and Sid were working away with Atlas, just starting the first cuts on a new location, when a Sheriff's Department Chevy Blazer pulled up to the jobsite and parked. Rippey saw them and backed the dozer off of the pad, then he idled the engine down for a minute and lowered the blade to the ground. When he climbed down from the open cab, a Sheriff's Deputy was standing with the SSA inspector. Officer Gibson had been a friend of Rippey for years. He looked like the classic western lawman with a weathered face and short graying hair. He respected John Rippey, and had the attitude that this was a clerical mistake conjured up by some city dwelling desk jockey.

"Hey, Rip, sorry to bug you," Gibson started. "This here is Inspector Farrow with the Social Security Administration in Denver. He'd like to ask you some questions if you wouldn't mind coming with us back to the station."

The inspector stepped closer. He wore khaki pants and a nylon windbreaker. "Hi there. Don Farrow." He shook hands with Rippey. "I do apologize for the inconvenience, I just need to run ID verification. You are Jonathon Tyler Rippey, correct?"

Rippey said, "That's me." with a slight gruffness creeping into his voice. Farrow continued with a smile, "Great! I just need to get some info, fingerprints and such. Then I can be on my way and this will all be sorted out."

"OK boys let's do this. The sooner we get there the sooner you'll see this is somebody's mistake," Rippey said and headed for the Blazer. Then he turned back to Sid, who had been standing quietly in the shade of the dozer, and called out,"Take care of Atlas and then head back to Joe's. We'll start fresh tomorrow." He shot a wink at Sid and Sid nodded. He watched them pile in the Blazer and drive off in a cloud of dust. Sid's eyes lingered as the dust faded away, and he tried to conceive of what he had just witnessed.

The next morning Rippey was talking in the back office with Joe. Relieved to see him, Sid assumed everything was back to normal.

That assumption lasted until Rippey walked out through the shop a minute later. He didn't say a word to the crew just grinned and gave a wave to the whole group. He stepped out the door, fired up his old Ford Bronco and drove away. Joe walked out and asked Sid if he flipped the battery disconnect when he left Atlas. Sid said he had. "Ahh good, thanks. You're going to work with Ronnie and Colin today ok?"

"Yeah, sure, Joe, that's fine. But is Rippey ok?" A look of distress flashed across Joe's face. "Yeah, he's just got some stuff to take care of."

For the next two days Sid worked with the other guys filling and compacting the soil around a newly poured foundation. They kept busy, but everyone speculated on what was really happening with Rippey. Joe was bouncing between the three work sites more than ever, like he didn't want to be at the office. He happened to be at the foundation site when a dark blue Mercury sedan pulled up. Two men got out, to Sid they both looked like John Elway in a suit. They walked up to Joe and asked if he was the owner of the company, when he said he was, they explained that they were U.S Marshalls looking for John Rippey and asked if he had seen him. Joe looked at the officers and told them, "I haven't seen him today, but he should be running the dozer at our Hall Ranch job."

Sid looked at the ground and dug a shovel into the soft earth, trying to do so quietly so he could still hear the conversation. One of the men gave Joe a card and asked him to call if he saw or heard from Rippey. They took down the address of the other work site, got in their car and drove off. Sid walked to Joe and could see the sadness filling the older man's eyes. "He's in big trouble, huh?"

Joe looked at Sid and replied, "When he left the other morning he told me, we would never see him again. I don't know what he's gotten himself into, but it looks pretty serious."

A grin crept across Sid's face as he looked at his boss. "I don't think they'll find any important clues at the dozer."

Joe gave a small laugh and shook his head, "No, probably not."

After work, Sid drove up the twelve miles of dirt road to Rippey's cabin and could see from the road that several unmarked cars as well as Sheriff's Department vehicles were parked in the driveway and people were coming in and out of the house. They also

92

had the work shop opened up and were going through it. Sid just drove past, then turned around and drove home.

When the news broke the next day, it washed over the town like a tsunami. John Rippey was not actually John Rippey. He had been living under a stolen identity since 1976, when he first came to town. His real name was Robert James Theabauld, and in 1975 he had been arrested in Nogales, Arizona smuggling forty-six pounds of marijuana across the border. He was indicted, and a trial was set for the following year. Then Theabauld posted an $18,000 bail bond and vanished.

With a stolen identity, John Rippey hitchhiked into a small mountain town, as it was slowly rebuilding itself and transitioning from a mining town into the ski resort destination it would become. He had plenty of opportunities for cash jobs and he quickly became embedded in the community. He eventually purchased an old mining claim in Irwin and built his house. Once he was established, he began devoting much of his free time to the community. He volunteered at the vet clinic and raised money for children's charity events. He helped to organize the Search and Rescue Service that was responsible for saving lost hikers and hunters every year.

When the locals learned that a drug smuggler living on the lam had tricked them, they were surprised, but not outraged. People in town all seemed to share the same idea that whoever he was, he had rehabilitated himself and paid for his crime through years of community service. News vans started arriving in town and reporters began combing the street seeking interviews from people who knew Rippey. The media wanted to paint the picture of a deceitful criminal hiding among the law-abiding citizens of this sleepy mountain town. Instead they quickly came to realize that the whole town supported him. Everyone reveled in the idea of a beloved local staying one step ahead of the law.

They recorded dozens of interviews, and each was a testimonial or anecdote that spoke about Rippey in a positive light. A woman from the Chamber of Commerce told how he had played Santa Claus for several years in the Christmas Parade. Then the fire chief from nearby Gunnison told about the wildfire four years ago that raged through the forest and into the edge of town. The Forest Service fire fighters were dangerously undermanned due to other large fires in

Summit County and the Western slope, so they enlisted the help of a few local heavy equipment operators to run machines and make a fire break in the thick forest to the north. Rippey ran a dozer tirelessly through the day and all that night clearing underbrush and pushing piles while the firefighters ran chainsaws to cut down trees. When the fire was contained, they determined thirty-five homes had been saved because of the noble efforts of those who worked that night, including Rippey.

The TV show America's Most Wanted tried to put together an episode about Rippey, but they too discovered that the little mountain town wasn't going to give up any drama about the friendly local everyone liked, even if he had committed a felony when he was younger. The fact was, Rippey may have been the most high profile fugitive to take refuge in C.B. but he certainly wasn't the only one. The town had a history of hiding draft dodgers and outlaws. Crested Butte was a quiet community that didn't ask questions, a place with a little bit of sunshine for people with a shady past.

The town may have forgiven him, but the DEA and the US Marshall's office had not. His case had officially reopened. In a statement given to the press, a DEA spokesman said, "Our department is not looking for John Rippey, we are looking for Robert Theabauld. We feel he still owes a debt to this country and we intend to make him pay. When he disappeared in 1975, he slipped through a system that was using paper files to trace criminals. We think he's going to find it much more difficult to escape this time."

16.

Eventually, life got back to normal. The guys got in more mountain bike rides, and they still went to work. Sid tried his hand at running Atlas the dozer, but found it to be much more difficult than one of the plush snowcats he was used to. For one thing, he steered the snowcat with one hand using two short control sticks. While on the dozer he had to steer using each of his feet to push in big pedals to release the drive clutches. He also discovered that dirt and stones were much harder to move around than snow.

In early September, Robert Theabauld was captured at the Canadian border near Bellingham, Washington and put in federal custody. The town of Crested Butte responded by throwing a Free Rippey Ralley. This started with chanting in a large mob on Elk

Avenue, and ended with partying late into the night. The bars donated a cut of their proceeds to a legal fund that Joe Green's wife had established. The owner of a coffee shop printed FREE RIPPEY bumper stickers and started selling them to donate to the cause. It had felt exciting to imagine Rippey moving on to a new town and setting up another new life for himself, but thinking of him now in an orange jumpsuit sitting in a cell was depressing. His capture united the town in an effort to support him, but it also brought a cloud of despair that could be seen on the faces of all those who knew the man.

The icing on the turd filled cake of a summer came in the form of a monsoon cycle. The guys were all jonesing to get in more mountain bike rides and the trails were primed. Each day they would make plans to ride after work, and each day would start out clear and warm all the way through lunch. Then around two o'clock dark clouds would roll in and burst open. For an hour the town would be pounded by torrential rain that always left the trails too muddy to ride.

Joneser knew the best way to get all his friends smiling again, he had a connection back home mail him ten hits of LSD in blue medical grade gel-tabs. He nervously retrieved them from his PO Box without any incident and brought them back to the apartment. The guys had only seen acid on blotter paper and were very impressed by the sleek blue bubbles still connected together in a straight row of ten. That Saturday Arliss joined them, as did Chrissy and Kevin. They all met at the local burrito shop and ate big, tasty burritos and a bowl of chips and salsa. Cliffy mentioned that this might be their last meal of the day. Joneser smiled and said, "You never want to eat on an empty stomach."

They finished lunch and walked to a big park a few blocks away and sat at a wooden picnic table. Joneser carefully cut seven hits apart with a small knife. Once each person had one, they popped it onto their tongues and smiled. Arliss was carrying a small backpack with a Nalgene water bottle, some sunscreen and a bag of dried cranberries. He encouraged his friends to put on some sunscreen, then he pulled a nice white Frisbee from the bag.

He twirled the Frisbee on his finger and told the others, "Watch this." The bright, warm afternoon sun glinted off the disc as it spun around and within a minute the special color changing plastic had transformed the disc into a deep purple.

"Whoa, this is the most fast-acting acid I've ever eaten," Cliff said.

"Oh my gosh! That is the coolest thing ever," Chrissy said with a surprised reaction. Sid always noticed that Chrissy never swore, and instead of making her sound naïve, he felt it actually made her sound much more intelligent than most of the other people he knew.

They walked out onto the large grass field and started throwing the disc around. Gradually everyone got in the groove and found the ideal distance from one another. Soon people were throwing trick shots and catching the Frisbee between their legs or behind their backs. Kevin had a technique of hurling it far off to the side, making it look like he had completely missed the target. But he would throw it up at such a steep angle that when it gradually stopped climbing and began to arc back to earth it would slice right down to the person he was aiming for. Cliffy and Joneser figured out how to ricochet the disc off the grass and have it bounce up to the catcher, but they quit doing that once it was apparent that it was chewing up the edge of Arliss's new disc.

Slowly a warm tingling sensation seeped into each of them, and they knew the trip had begun. Cliffy was the first to acknowledge it by saying, "Well, guys, I hope you didn't have any big plans for the next eight hours."

"All aboard!" Kevin called out. They kept throwing the disc, but the focus of the game changed. No more messing around. Now the object was to keep a long streak of throws and catches without dropping it. Everyone started throwing with laser precision, incredible dives were made to make the catch at all costs. The trip began to intensify and the group decided to take a break from the Frisbee. Arliss stashed it in his pack and passed his water bottle around.

They left the field and walked to an adjacent sand-covered playground. No one else was there so Kevin, Chrissy and Johnny chose swings at the tall metal swing set and each began pumping their swings higher and higher. Sid and Arliss just sat down at a bench on the side, while Cliffy and Joneser squatted down on a child-sized seesaw. Gentle seesawing quickly escalated into a death match with Joneser trying to smack his end on the ground violently enough to bounce Cliffy off his end of the plank. Cliff retaliated and the seesaw battle continued until each of them had been knocked off onto the sand at least once.

Sid and Arliss slouched back on the bench and tipped their heads back. The clouds welcomed them into a fluffily pleasant psychedelic state. Gazing at the clouds, Sid said to his friend, "I can't believe people go through life without experiencing this. It should really be mandatory."

"If enough people did this," Arliss explained, "the whole system would fall apart. No one would want to fight a war, no one would work themselves to death just to buy a bigger house. There wouldn't be any racism or hatred…"

"AHHH!" Cliffy's cry interrupted Arliss's thought. He and Joneser rode small animal figures mounted on thick springs stuck into the ground. They were much too heavy for the toys, so they rocked back and forth violently trying to crash into each other. Joneser slapped at Cliffy's hands hoping he would fall off, each of them laughing. Sid and Arliss watched them, then Arliss said, "Well, maybe there would still be wars, but at least they would be a lot funnier to watch."

Someone looked back across the field and noticed flashing red and blue lights in the late afternoon sun. One of the town cops had a car stopped on the side of the road, probably for exceeding the 15 mph limit in town. "I wonder if we can get in trouble for loitering in the kids' playground?" Chrissy asked the group.

Cliff answered her loudly, "Probably not as much trouble as we would for tripping our faces off in a public place."

"DUDE!" Johnny called out, "You are so loud, do you want them to hear you?" Cliff looked across the playing field at the parked police car and back at Johnny with a huge eye roll.

"Johnny, how are they going to hear me? Do you think they are sitting there with a Whisper 2000?" At this comment everyone burst out laughing. They had all seen the cheesy commercial that was in heavy rotation on the TV. It depicted elderly people struggling to hear conversations or the sound in a movie theater, so for only $19.95 they could buy a miraculous hearing device that consisted of a microphone and a pair of headphones. The thought of the police force using them to eavesdrop on citizens seemed particularly funny at the moment.

"Maybe we should head back to the A frame. It will start getting cold pretty quick," Kevin offered. They all agreed and started walking as the shadow of the mountain fell across town. Back at their house Arliss was selecting CD's from a rack and holding them up for Sid to decide on. Sid saw an excellent Pink Floyd album and called out,"Yes, play Meddle!"

Chrissy was putting away some clutter and misheard him. "No, I don't want to hear any metal. Play something lighter."

To which Joneser held up double devil horns and said, "YES! Metal! Put on some Ozzy!"

"No you dope, I'm not playing Ozzy. I'm putting on Pink Floyd." Arliss snapped at Joneser as he set the disc in the tray and closed it. Then he hit play and the sound of howling wind filled the room, followed by the reverberating bass of the first track. Chrissy felt energized and began organizing things in the kitchen. Cliff, Kevin and Joneser went up into the loft where a Sony Playstation was set up. Johnny, Arliss and Sid each found comfortable places to sit in the living room, right in front of the stereo. One small lamp provided light through a heavy shade as the orange sunset glowed from the window.

While the Floyd CD played, the three guys chatted a bit about the acid, then about Pink Floyd, then about other trips they had enjoyed. But the conversation gradually died down and each of them retreated back into their seats and closed their eyes. The first 'pings' of the twenty-three minute song 'Echoes' came out of the speakers. Sid melted into the couch, and he knew he wasn't going to move or open his eyes for the next twenty-three minutes.

Fractals of color spun in his vision, pulsing with the music, then slowly fading away leaving only darkness. Out of the darkness he felt himself moving through space. Not that he felt his body flying, but he possessed a new point of view, like a camera panning. Below him he saw a rounded tube, like a thick cable, and he was moving along parallel to it. The view pulled in close as it streamed along below, then his view perforated the outer surface of the tube and entered the interior.

A scene appeared, and Sid saw himself and childhood friends, at age thirteen all riding skateboards on an eight foot tall plywood half pipe. He remembered how he and his friends would taunt each other ruthlessly until one by one they each worked up the nerve to drop in to the steep, kinked transition. It was the most intense thrill Sid had felt to that point in his life.

The view broke the out of surface of the tube again and continued along. The tube stretched on ahead of him as far as he could see. Way off in the distance he could see a large sphere on the tube, and others behind it like a string of pearls. But before he got there, the view dove beneath the surface again. He instantly recognized the rickety double chair of Mohawk Mountain Ski Area. He was riding it at night, with Ethan Bennet a high school ski buddy. Beneath them, skiers scraped along the icy slope under the bright lights. Ethan wanted to be a singer for the band GWAR, but he claimed he wouldn't really need to sing. He could just make loud deep voiced screams, so that is what he practiced, screaming into the night as they rode up the chair.

"Man, that kid was funny," Sid thought, and then, POP, he was out on the surface of the tube, heading for the first sphere. A shudder ran through Sid as the realization hit him that he was looking at a record of his life, all his life experiences were contained within the tube that flowed past him. As he neared the first giant sphere, he noticed that is was not something on the tube, like a pearl on a string, instead it was a spot where the tube bulged out almost three times it's normal diameter. Curiously he entered the first flare, what could have made his life experience expand like this?

The scene opened and he saw himself with friends Shawn, Chris and Carrie floating on old black inner tubes down the Housatonic River. It was shortly after high school graduation. He remembered that day as the first time he had ever eaten acid. The river had never looked so beautiful while they spent the day lazily floating for miles. He was yanked from the memory and rushing along the tube again, he passed over a few of the bulges then dove into another one.

Oh, wow… he was in a warehouse in Denver, pulsing techno music flooded out from a wall of speakers. Lasers traced patterns onto the ceiling in time with the music as thousands of kids danced elbow to elbow in the vast, crowded building. He saw girls with blue eyeliner in knee-high striped stockings, and a boys in wide pants six sizes too large, all sweating and dancing. He looked up above the crowd to an elevated platform. Like a minister performing a sermon, the DJ held total control over the dancers. The alter in front of him held two spinning turntables. The earphones resting around his neck commanded the same respect as the collar of a preist. The music was pounding five separate tracks all layered and looped together perfectly like focused chaos. The DJ, however, stood serenely amidst the madness he had concocted. He flipped through vinyl records in a milk crate knowing the spirit would guide him to the sickest beats.

It dawned on Sid that if each of the life expanding bulges in the timeline represented a psychedelic experience, then probably the next dozen would be very similar to this rave-ZIP! Again his view sped over the timeline. As he expected, it skipped many of the bulges, before entering into one again.

Sid stood in front of a raging bonfire. It was chilly and he stood grinning ear-to-ear watching the flames lick at the night sky. He was in the mountains now, and this was Crested Butte's Vinotok, the pagan festival of the autumn solstice. The idea of the bonfire was to throw your bad mojo from the previous year onto it, and enter the winter with a clean slate. Some people threw hand written letters into it. Others tossed in old, damaged skis. The skis burned colorfully as the fiberglass and plastic ignited into blue and green flames. The crowd cheered with feral intensity. Sid looked around the crowd and saw grins and dilated pupils on half the locals around him, young and old alike. The timeline was getting caught up now; he figured this had to be the Vinotok from only last year. He became flushed with anticipation. Would this crazy trip show him the future?

When he was over the timeline again he looked ahead as far as he could. He saw the bulges become fewer and more spread out, but he saw something else: a branch right below him. It looked like it would have been a perfect split, a fork in the timeline, only it was a broken off stub still sparking like a snapped power line. Before he could consider it any longer he dove into it.

The scene materialized and he was laying on his back upside down looking up at one ski stuck into the snow. The tail of the ski broke free from the snow and he rapidly slid across the ice, his gloved fingers clawing frantically and finding no purchase. He felt his shoulders scrape across the narrow ribbon of rock as he went backwards off the edge. He heard the metal of his ski spark off the stone as it cleared the lip of the cliff. Then he heard only wind in his ears and a scream being ripped from his throat!

Johnny and Arliss sat engulfed in bliss as the song reached its instrumental crescendo right before the last verses of lyrics come back in. Arliss nodded his head rhythmically, a crooked finger tapping in the air and his eyes closed. Johnny was sitting in a lounge chair with each hand gripping an armrest. His head tilted back looking at the tapestry pinned to the ceiling. When Sid violently jolted upright it startled both of them. Sid sat up so fast he hit his head on the angled wall of the A frame. Johnny watched it happen and was concerned for half-a-second, then immediately found it really funny and started laughing hysterically. Sid was confused and rubbed his head. Arliss asked, "What the hell man, are you bugging out or what?"

Sid tried to form some words, "I…uh…I should be dead," he said quietly. Arliss cocked his head and raised an eyebrow, "Ok buddy, let's just sit down and take it easy." Sid sat down, his face flushed with embarrassment. Johnny was still giggling. Sid took a deep breath and let it out. He turned to Arliss with a vacant expression and said, "Whoa, that was intense."

Chrissy heard the commotion and came in. Ever the hostess; she had just brewed some tea and asked the guys if they wanted any. Arliss and Sid both accepted the offer, and she left to get it. Johnny regained his composure enough to ask, "Did you think a spider was on you or something?"

"No, it wasn't like that," Sid said, rubbing his eyes with both hands. "It was just…really…deep you know?"

"Yeah, I get it man," Arliss said in a soft calming tone. Trying to shift the focus off of his now self-conscious friend, he segued into a story.

"Jumping from a spider reminds me of some friends I have in Breck. These three couples went camping together and all ate mushrooms. They had the whole camp set up and a campfire going. They had dragged a big log over to sit on next to the fire. Right as the 'shrooms are really kicking in someone realizes that the log they are sitting on is full of ants, and by now the ants are all over them! I guess it was terrible. They were like, tearing their clothes off and freaking out." Johnny and Sid listened intently. Sid shook his head. "That sounds truly awful." A roar bellowed down from the loft. The guys upstairs were getting rowdy with whatever video game they were playing. Everyone could noticeably feel that the trip had peaked and was starting to wind down. It was only eight p.m. so with any luck they might still get a full night of sleep.

17.

102

A few nights later Johnny, Joneser, Cliffy and Sid were sitting in the apartment getting high. Cliffy had saved some money and purchased a red acrylic Graffix bong. He stuck a sticker on it that had a picture of Smokey The Bear and the words, Smoky's Helper. But the others had already started calling it Clifford the Big Red Bong. Pearl Jam's debut album was playing through in its entirety and the guys were talking about fitting a few more mountain bike rides in before winter hit. They knew the days were numbered. Snow had already shown up on the high peaks a few times.

"We should go to Moab or Fruita," Joneser declared. He was wearing a printed T-shirt that read, "I Love a Parade" over the image of a sniper lying in the prone position.

"Fruita is way closer," Johnny said, "and I've heard the trails are awesome. Maybe not as good as Moab, but still really good."

Cliffy noticed that Sid was zoning out and he threw a magazine at him, Sid winced and looked up at Cliffy, "What do you think Sid? Which place has better trails?"

"Uhhh, I wasn't listening."

"Yeah, no duh," Johnny said. "Dude, you've been out of it since the A frame. What happened when you were sitting there tripping?"

This piqued the interest of Joneser and Cliff. Joneser asked, "Yeah what happened? When the doors of perception were cleansed did you see things as they truly are?"

Cliffy chuckled at the comment and high fived his friend. "Nice one!" Joneser was paraphrasing a line from the author Aldous Huxley that Jim Morrison had used to name his band.

"Seriously dude, were you wigging out?" Cliff asked, "It's ok. I once went into a Coors Beer sign. Not like I bumped into a it, but I was trippin' at a friend's house, and there was this old Coors sign with a scene of the mountains and a big waterfall, and I actually felt like I was in the scene, sitting next to the river and I could hear the roar of the waterfall… Was it like that?"

"No you guys. It was just more like a vision," Sid started. "Like, it really hit me that if Rippey hadn't saved me I definitely would have slid off of that cliff. I would seriously be dead right now if it weren't for him. And now he's sitting in jail for something he did over twenty years ago, something that none of us would even consider a real crime. I feel like I owe a debt to him." The others were listening intently, and could tell Sid was serious.

"So what can we do for him, break him out of jail?" Joneser suggested.

"No, I already talked to Ellen Green, Joe's wife. She's the one who is organizing the defense fund. She said he just needs a really good lawyer to get his sentence dropped and that will take lots of money. She said anything I can do to raise funds would be the best use of my effort."

Cliff started loading the bong again and passed it to Johnny. "I wish my Dad could help, but he does corporate law, not criminal."

"Sucks for you," Johnny taunted.

"Yeah, I know, why couldn't he be a marijuana defense lawyer?" said Cliff.

"Corporations are the biggest criminals in the country." Joneser added for no real reason. He turned back to Sid "So what do you think you want to do? Hold a bake sale?"

"Maybe I'll sell my sled." The others looked at Sid in disbelief. Johnny blew out a big smokey hit and started coughing.

Joneser scoffed, "That sounds more like a *baked sale*. That's the dumbest thing I've ever heard, especially considering you owe like three times what it's worth. You've only had it two years on a five year finance, plus it's already beat to hell!"

"It's not beat to hell!" Sid said defensively.

"Yeah right, every piece of plastic is cracked and that one ski is mangled."

"That's just cosmetic damage."

"Fine, *expensive* cosmetic damage."

"Ok, OK, so selling the sled is a bad idea," Johnny said, stopping the pointless argument. "What else you got?"

"I'll sell my car," Sid stated as a matter of fact. The other three immediately laughed and groaned.

Joneser sat back in the chair shaking his head, "Pffft, for what? Two-hundred bucks? No offense, but that car looks like an abandoned vehicle. And then what, you'll take the bus to work or walk?"

"Two-hundred bucks would still be something." Sid countered.

"It won't make any difference to Rippey's lawyer." Johnny said.

"Well, you guys have been really helpful so far!" Sid exclaimed, "What do you suggest? I rob the Gas Cafe?"

"No, robbing a gas station two blocks from where we live is probably a bad idea." Joneser admitted.

"So, gas stations are out, what then? A bank?" Sid was getting wound up and snarky.

"No, we'd get shot," Joneser said quietly and calmly.

"Oh, *WE*, now?" Sid's voice raised an octave. "I've got a team? Ok then, an armored car?"

"Again, shot." Johnny said.

Joneser sat upright and held out his fist. "So ideally, we want, *One*," he extended his thumb, "to not get shot," he extended his pointer finger. "*Two*, a decent chunk of change. *Three*, a clean getaway."

"Really? Getting away warrants its own finger?" Johnny asked.

Joneser just looked at him blankly and continued. "*Four*, clean money, nothing with a paint bomb or shit that can be traced."

"You know, it sort of doesn't matter if it ends up being traceable, because it will all just be anonymously donated into the Free Rippey Fund," Johnny said. "I mean, its kind of a good plan, because lots of times the robbers get caught when they spend the money. But if the money just gets immediately dumped, then even if it turns out it's traced, it won't be connected back to us."

"Wow, Johnny, you're really getting into this," Sid said, nodding his head and looking impressed.

Johnny mildly laughed it off. "I mean this is just a thought experiment by four stoners. It's not like we would really do anything like this."

Joneser cleared his throat and bobbed his hand with four fingers up, "For *five*," he extended his pinky, "If possible, the target should be someone who deserves it, kind of a Robin Hood type scenario." No one responded for a moment, and the silence was broken by smoke bubbling through bong water as Cliffy filled the pipe. He exhaled through his nose, pulled out the slide, and inhaled deeply, filling his lungs to capacity with strong pot smoke. He held it in for a few seconds, snorted some out his nose like a dragon, and then blew a cloud up above their heads. With his eyes watering and glassy, Cliff said in a rough voice, "I know just the place."

All eyes focus on Cliffy as he explained, "Well, first off, if they fixed the glitch, then this idea won't work."

"Who? What Glitch?" Johnny asked anxiously.

Cliffy smiled, "Aspen Mountain."

He looked at Sid. "Remember when we went to the ticket booth and they were cash only? Do you know how much cash must pile up in there on a busy morning if they can't run credit cards?"

Johnny then asked, "Well, how would you know when their credit card machine isn't working? I have no idea when the one at the store is going to take a shit, typically it only happens when I have some asshole gaper trying to buy a tube of sunscreen."

"We would know exactly when it was going to crash. We would know months ahead of time," Sid answered, a look of stunned realization crossing his face. "It crashes when they hold big events, like races and mogul comps."

"Aspen is holding the X Games next February for the first time," Joneser said.

"Oh my god," Sid covered his mouth with his hand, then pulled it away, "When they held it here it was total chaos, remember? They rented every sled in the area so that film crews and athletes could be shuttled around the mountain."

"And there's your getaway," Cliff said, holding out his open palm towards Sid. Joneser looked down at the floor and shook his head chuckling. His black greasy hair waved like the tendrils of a jellyfish. He raised his head and his cheeks flushed with an enormous grin. "Are you guys saying we can rob the ticket booth at Aspen Mountain, a place that I hate with all my heart, then escape on sleds back to C.B?"

"No one is saying anything yet," Sid said. He looked at Joneser and Johnny, then his eyes settled on Cliff. "Cliff, have you been thinking about this ever since you saw that sign?" Sid asked, suddenly curious.

"Well, yeah. I was just wondering how much cash might be in there. So I went and talked with Shannon, the girl at the bakery. She works the ticket office here in winter. I asked her how many people buy day tickets. She told me that the supervisors bought them all pizza when they hit 5,000 tickets one day. Normally it's more like 3,500-4,000."

"And how much is a day ticket? C.B. is $42. Are Vail and Aspen are up to $47?" Sid asked. Johnny answered, "No, they *were* $47. This year they are bumping up to $50!" This was news to the other three who reacted with outrage.

"Fifty bucks for a day ticket? Who would pay that?" exclaimed Sid.

"It's part of the Snow Corp buy out. Eventually they will raise tickets on all their resorts." Johnny explained.

"They need to be robbed as a form of protest," Joneser declared. "Like when the Earth Liberation Front burned down that new lodge at the top of Vail, to protest the resort's expansion."

"I think they all got caught too," Cliff added somberly. "Dumb hippies."

"Stealing $150,000 cash, is a hell of a protest statement." Johnny said.

"Oh shit, is that how much it could be?" Sid asked.

"Well, if you figure low at 3,000 day tickets times fifty bucks each, that's $150,000," Johnny explained. "Each ticket is actually more with sales tax, but I really doubt they would just let that much cash pile up in the ticket booth. They probably are supposed to dump it into a floor safe or something."

"They are *supposed* to," Cliff cut in. "But these are minimum wage seasonal employees we're talking about. If it's a busy morning, I bet they get behind on making drops."

"That is a risk," Joneser said, "but I'm willing to bet against low level seasonal employees doing their job exactly as it's required."

"That raises another question," Sid said. "When do you try something like this? Do you try it before nine a.m. when the lines at each window go back fifty feet, or wait until after ten, when most of the windows have closed and you just have a few stragglers buying tickets? When it's crazy early in the morning, there's a better chance the cashiers haven't made their drops, but you also have over a hundred people all watching what you are doing. What if there's an off duty cop standing in line?"

"Definitely late morning," Joneser stated with assurance. "There is no way we could control a maze full of bystanders."

"How would you even control the cashiers?" Johnny asked doubtfully. "You think you can just walk to the window and look threatening?"

"Yeah, Joneser should wear his barbarian costume from last Halloween!" Sid laughed. "I heard that if you use a gun without bullets it's less of a crime than using a loaded one."

"Sid, you heard that on Raising Arizona." Cliffy said.

"Oh, yeah I did." Sid said, feeling a little dumb.

"I think guns would be a bad idea," Cliffy said as he stood up. He walked to the fridge and pulled out four cans of Pabst Blue Ribbon. As he walked back to the living room, he continued. "None of us owns a gun or even knows how to use one. I think we could take control of the ticket booth with something that's disorienting, but nonlethal, like a smoke bomb or something."

"I doubt it would take much," Sid added as he popped the top on his beer and took a sip. "Getting robbed is going to be the last thing some ticket booth cashiers are ever expecting."

"Ooooooh, I know just the thing, bear spray!" Johnny said as he broke into an evil grin. "We sell it at the shop, and it would be perfect, because you could shoot it through the little hole in the window."

"Damn, Johnny, that's a good idea," said Cliff as a toothy smile lit up his face. "I bet if you filled the ticket office with bear spray, the cashiers would run out the backdoor. If we were there waiting, we could just walk right in."

"But then we would need to be protected from the spray," Sid said as he considered the scenario. "We could have like, gas masks or something."

Joneser joined the brainstorming session again. "We would need to test this system before we actually do it. That would really suck if we ended up incapacitating ourselves with our own bear spray."

Joneser pulled the slide from the bong and tapped the ash into an empty beer can. He packed the bowl full of green bud and picked a blue Bic lighter off the table. He held the lighter in his hand and as if he were examining a hard piece of dogshit. "I hate these fucking childproof lighters."

Joneser pulled the old spoke poker out of the drawer and fished it under the strap of metal covering the roller on the lighter. The metal sprung loose from the lighter and fell to the table. Joneser put the spoke down and gleefully flicked the lighter a couple times, proud that he had disabled the safety strap and rendered the lighter non-childproof.

As Joneser cleared the bong Sid looked to his friends and asked, "If this actually happened, would you guys really do this just to donate the money to Rippey? You guys don't owe him like I do. If we somehow stole $150,000 split four ways that's... uh, 75 is half, 30...35 plus some, so over $35,000 for each of you. You guys wouldn't need to donate your share. That's like a down payment on a house here in town."

Johnny spoke up with a look on his face like he had just caught his dad masterbating."Sid, come on man! Really? None of this is serious. Rippey made his own choices. He led a life of crime, he wanted to run drugs and make a shit ton of money. He got away for a while, but then he got caught. He is not your responsibility. Were you actually thinking of doing this stupid shit? For real?"

Sid looked at him stoically: "Yes."

"Jesus," Johnny said.

"If we tried this idiotic plan, we would get caught. We would be sent to prison! You want to live in Colorado for the rest of your life? How about a federal prison in Buena Vista or Canon City? Spit was flying from Johnny's mouth as he unleashed his tirade at Sid, Sid shrunk from his friend and his expression changed from shock into shame. "Yeah that sounds nice." Johnny raged "Just think, when this stupid plan fails, you will be ass raped by the Aryan Brotherhood, you will be someone's bitch! Maybe you could have a cell right next to Rippey your hero!"

Sid slid deeper into the couch as he tried to replay the night's events and understand at what point he had coerced his best friends into committing a felony. Wait, had he coerced them? Sid thought. Didn't Cliffy have the idea?

Sid's train of thought was broken as Joneser spoke calmly and deliberately. He stared straight at Johnny and the psychotic look in his eye became unmistakable.

"Johnny, you don't need to have anything to do with this. All you need to do is just shut the fuck up, and never speak a word about what you've heard."

"Seriously Johnny," Cliffy said, "Way to be a major buzzkill. We don't need you in here going off about," Cliff held his fingers up in air quotes, "'*Laws*' and '*Assrape.*' Johnny if you don't want to be involved that's fine. Besides there are only two sleds, and I'm not riding bitch on a crazy snowmobile getaway chase, so really it would only be these two retards doing the actual robbery anyway." He held his hand out to Sid and Joneser. "I'm just going to be *an accomplice,* as they say."

Sid couldn't believe what he was hearing. His friends were much more unhinged than he had ever expected. "Cliff, why on earth would you ever risk fucking up your life like this?"

Cliff folded his hands together and drew in a deep breath as he looked at Sid. "My father is one of the most successful lawyers in the state- for all I know, the country. He works his ass off and makes a ton of money. And he is the most boring, unhappy person I have ever met. He drives a BMW that is designed to do 180mph on the Autobahn and he goes 50 on Interstate–fucking-70. He's out of shape, his hair is falling out, and by the American standard, *HE IS SUCCESSFUL*! Everything I've done at CU so far has been pre-law shit, and my family thinks I'm just here in C.B. for a few seasons to 'get it out of my system' before I go back to school and become just like him. Well, I don't want to, and nothing I tell my family can make them understand that. If my father is successful, then I want nothing to do with it. I want to do something real with my life."

"And you think throwing your life away to sit in jail would really teach your parents a lesson?" Johnny asked, his voice dripping with cynicism.

"Johnny, we wouldn't try it if we didn't think we could pull it off. The X Games are in February. That gives us four months to prepare. And if anything falls through, right up to that moment, we call it off and walk away," Joneser explained.

Johnny looked at Joneser. "Why the hell would you want to be involved in this? I can't believe it would purely be revenge for screwing you out of a season pass? I know you are a deranged sociopath, but you do understand the consequences, right? You know that you would not do well in prison?"

"Johnny, for one thing, I would not let them take me alive. Also, I think this is a perfect way to send a message to these ski areas that think they can raise prices every year, put blackout dates on out season passes, and keep us in indentured servitude. They keep paying us pennies, while they just grow richer and richer."

"Wow Hayduke, that sounds really noble." Cliffy said referencing the outlaw god of the Monkey Wrench Gang. Cliff wasn't buying Joneser's explanation one bit. "Really? You only want to do this as a sign of protest? You don't want to keep any money for yourself because you enjoy living in poverty?"

"Yeah," Joneser admitted guiltily. He looked at Sid like he was asking permission. "I really want to keep enough for a down payment on a place. That's the only way I could ever make it happen. I think I could use the stolen cash to pay rent here and live on for a year or two. I'd just save my paychecks in the bank, until I had enough to put down."

"Dude, I think you should," Sid responded. "I think each of you should use your share however you like, as long as you don't get caught with it. I'm the only one with a life debt to repay. And like Cliffy said, you and I would be playing the riskiest part, pulling the actual robbery." Sid turned to his friend with a pleading expression, "Johnny, you and Cliff would be behind the scenes. We could play this so that nothing ties you to the crime, but you could still get an equal share. Wouldn't you like to buy a place here in town too?"

Johnny thought it over. He felt each of his friend's eyes on him awaiting a response. Then, he reluctantly joined the cabal. "Alright, as long as I'm not directly involved. I'll be a lookout or something."

"Fuck yeah." Cliffy held out his beer, then Joneser and Sid each joined him, clinking the cans together. Johnny slowly clinked his against the others, and Cliffy said, "To the best, or possibly worst, decision of our lives." They crashed the cans together and cheap beer spilled to the table. Each of them chugged their beer and slammed down the empty can.

18.

Johnny decided not to work snow making again that year when the outdoor shop offered him a permanent position as a manager and helped him pay for a season pass. Soon he was bringing home topographical maps covering all the area between C.B and Aspen. He also stole a detailed map of the ski runs at Aspen that was printed on a cloth substance that felt like a dollar bill. The guys kept the maps and other information related to the heist in the bottom drawer of the dresser in the back bedroom. They only brought out one section of map to survey at a time, in case friends dropped by unexpectedly and saw it.

By the second week of November, Aspen Mountain turned on the lifts and started its new ski season. The guys were dying to know if there was any chance of their scheme working out. Cliff volunteered to call the Aspen Ticket Information office. He had in front of him a calendar of local ski events for the upcoming season. The phone rang and was swiftly answered as the others huddled around Cliff to listen in.

Cliff, for some reason, made his voice sound like a black comedian impersonating a white guy."Yes hello, my name is Matthew Jones. I had a question about ticket purchasing." Joneser hit him in the arm, and Cliff ignored it, staying focused. "Well, last season I brought my family to Aspen for vacation and we came while you were hosting a big mogul competition. I noticed when we bought our tickets they weren't accepting credit cards. If we come up the week of the fifteenth in February, I see you have the something called the X Games going on. Would I be able to use a credit card that weekend, or should I bring cash? Yes, I can hold." Cliff held the phone to the side and said to the guys, "He's going to ask his supervisor."

Joneser glared at him. "Really? You use my name when you need a fake name?"

"Relax, I only use it when I rent porn at the video store." He quickly held up his hand and put the phone to his ear. "Yes, I'm still here…ok…I see…great. Thank you. Yes, the four-pack does seem like a good deal…uh, huh…yes, are you actually raising the cost of a day ticket to $50? Doesn't that seem a little ridiculous? Did you make any improvements to the mountain? I would expect fur lined chair lift cushions for a $50 day ticket." The others giggled at Cliff's audacity, "Ok well, I do appreciate your help. Thank you…yes, you too."

Cliff hung up the phone and looked at the others with a devious smile. "You guys want to pull a heist?"

"Really? What did he say?" Sid asked anxiously.

"His manager told him that next summer they will be upgrading all their phone lines to fiber optic cable, so it will no longer be an issue. But, if we come this year we can expect to pay cash only. He apologized for the inconvenience and really the best thing to do would be to buy a four pack for my wife and kids."

"What did he say when you asked about the $50 tickets?" Johnny asked.

"Oh, he said, 'Fuck off, you'll pay it and you'll like it," Cliff answered.

"Holy shit," Sid said, he sunk back into the couch. His face looked grim. "I guess it's on?"

"Oh, it's on like Donkey Kong!" Joneser said grinning.

Sid knew that this scheme would take some extra money. He hand drew some fliers for his beacon, a pair of climbing skins he didn't use, and his mountain bike. He hung them at the grocery store's bulletin board, at the outdoor shop and one at each of the local bike shops. Within a week he had a few hundred dollars of extra cash. The other three agreed that when the heist paid off he should at least replace these items with new ones.

Sid and Joneser picked up both sleds from the trailhead and brought them to their friend's garage at the Whiterock Avenue house. The garage was dark and bitterly cold at night, but they borrowed some work lights and a small space heater from Sid's old employer Joe Green. The heater screamed like a jet engine and filled the small space with fumes instantly, but if they used it sparingly it took the edge off the freezing workspace.

Sid wanted to be certain that both sleds were in top shape if they were to become getaway vehicles. Together he and Joneser tipped the machines on their sides and pulled the rear suspensions out. They disassembled all the linkage, cleaned it and greased it. Once the rear suspensions were done, they tightened all the bolts in the steering linkages and went through the engines, tightening hose clamps and looking for leaks. They moved on to cleaning the clutches and inspecting the clutch weights and rollers.

Before they were all done, Sid had made another trip to Sun Power Sports in Gunnison for a new ski to replace his mangled one, and a set of weights and rollers for the clutch in Joneser's Polaris. He was nearly halfway through his money and this was just one part of the whole project. Joneser helped pitch in and bought an extra belt for each of the sleds.

Once all the repairs had been made to their sleds, Sid and Joneser took an electric grinder and ground off the numbers stamped into the aluminum tunnels of their machines. Each of them had a few layers of registration stickers built up on the hood. Together they peeled them off after heating them with a hair drier. Cliff stopped by the garage to see how they were doing.

As he stepped inside he grabbed his throat with his hand and pretended to gag, "Holy shit how can you guys even breathe in here? That thing stinks," he said pointing to the heater. Sid unplugged the heater and the blasting jet engine sound died away.

Joneser said, "Shut the door, you're letting all the pretty colors out."

"Yeah, I never liked those brain cells anyway," Sid added.

Sid started shaking a can of black spray paint and then painting over the area where the numbers had been ground off. Cliffy sat down on Joneser's sled and put his hands on the handgrips. "So are these ready for the big getaway?"

"I think so." Sid answered, dropping the hood shut.

19.

They were still discussing plans for the sled escape at the apartment as they passed around a joint and listened to the stereo playing on random. Joneser had one of his skis flipped upside down on the coffee table as he performed some damage control. On the base of his ski a long, jagged gash ran down the center. A frayed strip of material ran along the gouge. While his roomates floated dumb ideas for the robbery, Joneser focused on cutting away the material with a dull bayonet of unknown origin. He cut away the strip, held up a thin black rod of P-Tex and lit the end on fire with a lighter. The P-Tex sizzled and sparked as black, burning drips started to run off the end of the stick. Joneser leaned in and carefully drizzled the liquid into the gouge in his ski. Once the entire scratch was filled in, he blew out the stick and set it down on the table still smoking.

"It would be sweet if the sleds could change color, like the Lamborghini with the two hot chicks at the beginning of Cannonball Run." Johnny said with a stoney chuckle.

"Which Cannonball Run?" asked Sid.

"The one with Jackie Chan," Cliffy answered as a matter of fact.

"Wait, Jackie Chan was in Cannonball Run? Seriously?" Sid asked, confused.

"Definitely," Cliff said. "He might even be in both of them." The joint had been handed to him and he noticed the paper was burning too fast down one side. He wet the tip of his finger with his tongue and dabbed at the burned area to get the joint burning evenly again. "Him and another guy drove like, a Subaru and it was full of high-tech electronics gear."

"Oooh, no shit? I remember those guys," Sid said, as his mind absorbed this powerful realization. "But, he's not even Japanese…"

"Johnny!" Joneser said loudly to break the tangent and get back to what Johnny had mentioned. "So what is the color change trick?"

"You've never seen that movie?" Johnny cocked his head in disbelief.

"I think I've seen some of it," Joneser said. "He drives a race car and dresses like a chicken or some shit."

"Nope, that's Stroker Ace," Cliffy cut in. "Honestly, I'm appalled at your lack of Burt Reynolds movie knowledge."

"Fuck off Cliff," Joneser said, "I liked the one where he was a future cop who caught the out of control robots."

"Oh, my god?!" Cliff slapped his palm over his face, then pulled it down. "Dude, that wasn't even Burt Reynolds. That was Tom Selleck," he said with as much condescention as he could muster.

"What…The Fuck…Ever." Joneser said as he ran the knife down along his ski, removing excess drips. He pointed the blade at Johnny. "Tell me how they changed color!"

"Oh, yeah," Johnny snickered, "They had this blue Lambo, and they sprayed it with water and all the blue washes off and it's red underneath."

Joneser considered the idea. "Well, water based paint probably won't do us any good, but I like the idea. I bet I could come up with something." He held his ski up like he was aiming a rifle and looked down the length, satisfied with his repair.

20.
This product may be used only to deter bears which are attacking or appear likely to attack humans. Do not spray this product on objects, tents or humans; such use has *no* deterrent effect on bears. Do not seek out encounters with bears or

intentionally provoke them. "Wow, people are so dumb," Cliff said as he read the label on the canister. "This means that somewhere, somebody sprayed this on themselves thinking it worked like bug spray."

"It also means that somebody went out looking for a bear they could spray with it," Joneser added.

"Hopefully it was the same person," Johnny said and the others laughed. "Now this stuff is supposed to be pretty nasty." He held what looked like a miniature fire extinguisher. It was eight inches tall and bright red.

"You mean you haven't tried it yet?" Joneser asked. "How could you guys sell a product that you haven't personally tested?"

"Well, that's what we're here for today," Johnny countered.

They had driven Joneser's truck out to a secluded pulloff on a dirt road. Snow covered the ground and sun shined in through the trees. On the open tailgate sat two five-gallon buckets of water and a few old bathroom towels. They also had a gallon jug of drinking water, two cans of bear spray and an assortment of protective gear. Sid opened a bag containing a new respirator he had bought at the hardware store. He had told the clerk he was stripping paint from an old bike frame and wanted the best protection. The old man had sold him a respirator rated for chemicals and some clear plastic goggles you might see in a high school shop class.

Joneser's set up was much more impressive. After a theatrical pause and unzipping of his backpack, he produced a Vietnam War era M17 military gas mask he had bought years before to use as a Halloween costume. Joneser pulled his black hair out of his face and slid the mask over his head. The unit was made of black rubber and had filters built in to the thick sides that hung down like jowls. It had small circular vents on each side and one large round vent in the center. He looked out through two large glass eye holes. Straps running around his head held it all in place.

"Damn Joneser, you look like something from a nightmare," Johnny said.

"Even more than usual," Cliffy added.

Sid was inspecting his safety goggles and noticed vents running all around the outside of the lens. He was trying to cover the vents with black electrical tape, but the tape wouldn't stick. Cliff began looking at some old ski goggles they had brought and found a pair with vents that were easier to plug. They stuck the tape over the vents, and Sid put the dark, amber tinted goggles on with the respirator.

The other three immediately agreed that this was a much better look, stating that too much of his face was visible through the large clear safety goggles. Next, Sid and Joneser pulled on white Tyvek painting suits over their clothes and thin latex gloves. They pulled the hoods over their heads and walked out to the edge of the clearing about 20 feet away. Cliff pulled the safety tab from a canister and smiled with glee. Joneser spoke, his voice muffled through mask, "Just do a little bit at first to make sure we are ok."

"Why, are you starting to have doubts about the thirty-year-old filter in that mask?" Cliff asked. Then he squeezed the trigger of the can and a red stream of gas shot out forming a cloud around the two masked figures. Cliff held the trigger for two or three seconds, much longer than a short burst they had expected. The cloud of red dust swirled around them. Despite the respirators, both of them held their breath at first. Then slowly and cautiously, they began to draw air through the filters. When Joneser realized he could breathe through the filter he began a muffled yell through the mask, "Cliff you asshole, you were supposed to do a small burst, I'm going to kick yo...!"

PSSSSSSSSSSSSSSHHHHH!! Cliff fired another stream at Joneser, emptying the can. The cloud dissipated and Joneser lunged at Cliff, who dropped the empty canister and dodged the attack by running behind the truck.

"Can you feel it?" Johnny asked.

Sid responded, "Yeah, definitely. My neck feels like the worst sunburn you can imagine. It also burns between the goggles and the mask. My eyes sting, but they aren't watering too bad."

"I can feel it on my neck too," Joneser said. "It burns like hell."

"Can you see ok out of the masks?" Cliff asked, "Are they fogging up at all?"

"Not yet, but, we should move around and try breathing heavy through them, let's run up that embankment." Sid said pointing to the steep forty-foot bank across the road.

"Ok," Joneser said and he took off running. Sid followed close behind. They scrambled up the dirt hill kicking loose rocks and reaching down with their hands at times for a better grip. They reached the top and Sid doubled over. Joneser put both hands on the top of his head, each of them gasping for air through the restricting filters. Then -just as fast- they half jumped, half ran down the slope and raced up to Cliffy and Johnny. They stood there panting in white coveralls and facemasks, waiting to see if their lenses fogged over.

"You guys look like you're training for the pest control Olympics," Cliff observed.

"They don't look like they're fogging," Johnny said, leaning in close and inspecting the goggles and gas mask. "And we didn't even put any defogger on them."

"Should we hit them again?" Cliff said holding the second can of spray.

"Fuck no!" Sid said. "My neck and face are seriously on fire. I need to wash this shit off." He pulled the hood back and took off his goggles and mask.

"Besides that stuff is $35 a can. We don't need to waste it." Johnny said.

"It's not wasting it if it's for testing purposes, and besides, you stole it anyway. What do you care?" Cliff said to Johnny.

"You just want to spray me again you shit head," Joneser said as he walked up behind Cliff and squeezed one of his ears with his glove that was covered in red dust.

"Oh you bastard," Cliff said laughing as he pulled away from Joneser's grip.

Minutes later, Sid, Cliff and Joneser were all standing at the tail gate holding wet towels to their irritated skin.

Johnny asked, "So you think you could function, doing the hardest task of your life with some of that getting on your face?"

"Well," Sid responded, "With the mask and goggles, I'm not disabled. It's just painful."

"And what if you didn't get a chance to wash your face off?" Johnny continued, "What if you had to ride all the way back with your face burning?"

"If it goes as planned," Joneser said, "we won't even be exposed to that much spray. We really only need enough to scare the employees out of the ticket office. And I bet it won't take much."

"And I'll bring a pack of those baby wipes in my pocket," Sid said as he got the idea. "With those I could even clean my face while I'm riding."

When they finished wiping off their skin, they stuffed the suits and gloves into a garbage bag. Sid and Cliff climbed into the bed of the pickup truck for the ride back to town. Sid felt the fresh air blowing on his face and it felt good.

Later that week, Cliff, Joneser and Sid boarded the chairlift at the bottom of the Silver Queen terminal and started heading up to the top of Crested Butte Mountain. Cliff and Sid had both laid their ski poles down and sat on them as the lift came around. Joneser let his poles dangle by the straps from his wrists. The heist was becoming all they could think about. They tried to only talk about it in places where they couldn't be overheard, and the chairlift was a perfect spot.

"We still need to think of where the sleds could be parked," Sid said, he was sitting on the end of the chair and leaned forward so he could see Cliff next to him, and Joneser on the other end.

"What if we dropped them off at night, and hid them in a snow bank?" Joneser said.

"That might work, but you don't want to run out with two sacks of cash and then shovel the sleds out of a frozen snow bank. Plus we'd need to drop the sleds off in the middle off the night. Even then someone might see us," Cliff said.

"Maybe since the X Games are going on, we could put flags on the sleds and fleet numbers. Then just park them at the base and people would assume they belong to film crew or some other department," Sid said.

"That's true," Cliff agreed, "putting flags on your sleds might be a good idea. It will make them look less obvious as you race from the base area to the boundary. Maybe it will even prevent you from running over a skier on your way up the slope."

"Speaking of that," Sid said. "Do we even know that mountain well enough to find a good route up from the bottom? I know I wasn't paying attention to any trail names when we were there last time."

The upper terminal was only a tower away now- the ride was almost over. Sid pulled his poles out from under him and prepared to exit the chairlift. No one had responded to his question.

The chair reached the top and they all stood up in unison and skied down the ramp. Cliff pulled his goggles over his eyes and said to the others, "We need to go ski Aspen again."

21.

"Hi, how are you today?" Joneser asked the couple in their sixties as he approached. They were walking away from the ski area and headed towards the town of Aspen. The two wore matching white Bogner one-piece ski suits with fur trim that was definitely real. Joneser tried to look friendly with an exaggerated smile. The man protectively took a step in front of his wife.

"We are doing very well," the man said with the confidence of an extremely wealthy person. "Is there something I can help you with?"

Joneser wore his dirty ski jacket with duct tape patches, his hair slithered limply out from under an olive drab beanie. He looked like a derelict. "I was just wondering if you two were done for the day, and if so is there any chance that I could have your day tickets?"

The man's composure slipped into bitter annoyance. "We are season pass holders for one thing, and for another, what you are doing is illegal and if you continue to bother people, I will have you arrested."

Joneser's fake smile dropped into a sneer. "I really don't think it's illegal, so thanks anyway." Then he turned and walked back to see if Johnny and Cliff were having any luck. The man in white huffed and muttered something to his wife as they walked off. Joneser replayed the interaction in his mind to see where he went wrong. The skiers weren't carrying skis as they left the area, so he should have deduced that they had their own locker at the base lodge. But they could have been renting equipment, possibly? No, no one who owns a white fur lined one-piece suit, rents skis. He furrowed his brow and thought, 'Thanks anyway?' Did that even make sense as a comeback?

As he walked up he saw Johnny talking with two skiers who, incidentally, still wore their boots and held their skis and poles with them. Johnny handed one of them a twenty-dollar bill and carefully used his Leatherman tool to cut through the metal wicket that held a day ticket to the man's jacket. He removed the ticket and then did the same with the second man's ticket. Johnny thanked the men as they walked.

"Nice one,"Joneser said as he approached. "You did way better than I did, I had a guy try to throw me out."

"He was probably afraid of you. You didn't threaten him, did you?" Johnny asked.

Before Joneser could respond, Johnny explained, "Those guys came up from Denver and they had to head back this afternoon." He was hooking the cut wicket into a zipper on his coat and then sticking the cut end back into the fold of the adhesive so it would hold together without looking tampered with.

"Where's Cliffy?" Joneser asked, looking around.

"He went straight to the ticket booth. Said he wanted to check it out." The two of them walked up Durant Avenue past a posh ski shop full of designer ski wear. They looked across the main pavilion at the tiny ticket booth. The booth was a freestanding building nestled right next to a much larger building with condos in the upper floors and assorted shops along the ground floor. It was 10:30 and the booth had already closed two of its four windows. Two people stood together at one window, while the other had just one customer. The morning rush had died down, and there were still a few hours before the half- day tickets went on sale.

They looked around and spotted Cliffy sitting at a bench, sipping a paper cup of coffee and casually taking in the seen. From his vantage point he could observe three sides of the small ticket booth. They walked up and sat next to him, he grinned, "Did you guys score some tickets?" Johnny answered, "I got two, Joneser just scared people."

Cliff rolled his eyes, "Well that figures. Ok two is all we need anyway. I want to stay here and keep watching. Four people were working the windows earlier when it was busy, one just left from a door in the back, but he wasn't carrying anything. I'll try to find out if the money just stays in there throughout the day. You guys go up and work out the best route over the mountain. Remember, things might be different when it's all set up for the X Games. I'll see you guys this afternoon. Maybe I'll take a run if I think of anything I want to check out."

Joneser and Johnny got up and walked into one of the rooms under the Little Nell Hotel. They found rows and rows of lockers that skiers could rent. It cost seventy-five cents to lock and unlock the locker each time, so they just threw their street shoes into a locker with Cliff's boots and left it unlocked.

Cliff finished his coffee and unlatched the bear-proof trashcan. He dropped the cup in and let the lid slam. Then he walked to one of the ticket booth windows. A guy younger than Cliff greeted him through the glass partition. He wore a polo shirt with the Aspen Snowmass logo on one side of his chest. On the other was a gold nametag that read, 'Eric, La Salle, CO'.

"Hi there," Cliff said, "I was wondering if I could ask you a few questions?" Cliff then proceeded to hit him with a range of questions about ticket packages and which skis he should rent.

Eric was bored and naturally talkative, so he was happy to chat with Cliff while the few other customers dealt with his co-worker at the other window. While Eric went into detail on the benefits of capped skis and sidecuts, Cliff was sweeping his gaze around the interior of the small building. He took notice of the placement of two security cameras. He studied the cash registers at each station and tried to picture how a stream of bear spray would move through the small space. The shape of the building made it somewhat difficult to get a clear view of everything. Each ticket window was staggered farther in than the one next to it, like a set of steps tipped on their side. Cliff kept thinking it looked like a piece from the Nintendo game TETRIS. He leaned in close as if he was listening intently to the conversation and his eyes ran methodically over the floor, and … there it was: the cash drop box. Cliff saw a round metal door about twelve inches around set flush into the floor next to the back wall. It had a standard sized padlock on it and Cliff knew from experience that a large bolt cutter would make quick work of that lock.

"I hope that helps." Eric concluded.

"It does, thank you," Cliff said walking off. He easily blended in with the other tourists. As the Aspen ski area bordered the edge of town, it was normal to see people just wandering around the pavilion, looking in shop windows and taking in the view. Cliff walked away from the ski area and crossed Durant Avenue. He turned and looked at the area from a distance, how on earth would the guys be able to get from the ticket booth to the sleds, and then how would the sleds get to the snow? This was a serious logistics question he needed to answer.

He reached in his pocket and pulled out Johnny's wooden one hitter box, he dug the pipe into the stash of shake weed, discretely held the pipe like a cigarette and took a big pull off of it. He put the box away and looked back across the intersection. Crossing Durant again he meandered around the Little Nell Hotel building. As he turned down Spring Street he noticed a small parking area in front of the loading dock doors marking the service entrance to the hotel. He walked a little further down Spring Street and a dopey smile spread across his face.

Johnny and Joneser stood at the top of Aspen Mountain. The gondola had let them off at an elevation of 11,212 feet. Behind them was the Sundeck and behind that was the ski area boundary leading to what would be their escape. Below them lay the town and the ticket booth. The two of them stood in front of a large 10-foot by 10-foot trail map. They had already spent hours debating the best probable route up the mountain. They had also considered heading straight out of the ski area and neither side looked very promising. If they ducked out of the ski area they would be boondocking through deep untracked snow. Attempting that carried a high risk of getting stuck and allowing the ski patrol ample time to fan out from the ski area and begin a search. Since they would be slogging through the woods, the tracks they made could be followed right to them.

If they came through the ski area, they could ride on hard packed ski runs. With a clear path the sleds could reach maximum speed. Also they would not leave a very distinguishable track on the busy, tracked out slope. If they could reach the boundary at the top, they would have a very short section of boondocking, before they gained access to the network of heavily ridden trails that would eventually lead back to C.B.

The mountain did have a natural path straight up the middle on a series of blue runs, but this section would be the main venue for the X Games. Their objective would be to develop a path up the west side of the ski area. While making ski runs down the slopes on that side, they would frequently stop and make notes on their maps indicating temporary fencing or other obstacles. A few sections of roped off service roads looked particularly interesting. Service roads would be ideal, because no skiers would be on them and the snowcats that travel them at night keep them hard packed and buttery smooth.

Joneser and Johnny stood at the entrance to one of these roads, an orange nylon rope hung across the road and a sign showed the international sign for no skiers. It would be illegal by Colorado law to duck the rope and go under, but they had to know if this access road was the shortcut they were looking for. Joneser pulled out his trail map, took another glance at it and stuffed it into his pocket. "Let's go down, I think I know a way we can get on that road."

Ten minutes later they were riding up side by side on a double. The chairlift slowly crept past a Douglas fir draped in colorful shimmering Mardi Gras beads that had been thrown from the lift over the years. Past the tree an access road came into view crossing directly under the chair. "I think that's the same road." Joneser said.

"OK, how do we get on it?" Johnny asked. Then as the chair crossed over the road, Joneser slipped his glove from his hand and let it silently fall to the snow-covered road. Someone in the chair behind them called out loudly, "OOOOOHHHH!" Another rider mimicked the trombone sound of, "Wahhh, Wahhhhhhhh!" Johnny smiled as he realized Joneser's plan. At the top they exited the lift and looked around for some ski patrol, but none could be seen. So they told the lift attendant they needed some help getting the fallen glove. He went into his little booth and picked up a phone.

A few minutes later a ski patroller skidded to a stop next to them. He raised his goggles and exposed a goggle tan so extreme he looked like a raccoon. "What's up guys?" he asked with a slight California surfer drawl. Joneser explained how he had dropped his glove while trying to wipe his goggles and asked if he could go get it. The patroller considered it for a second and then agreed to take them down the access road. When they got there, he even held up the orange rope to allow Johnny and Joneser to duck under it. Together they skied under the lift. Joneser grabbed his glove and put it back on. The patroller led them to the lower end of the road. Again, he held up the rope for them and they skied out onto a ski run. They thanked him and looked around to get oriented. They were delighted to see they were a few thousand feet straight up from the base area. The service road would function as a perfect short cut, as long as they could get safely under the ropes.

Back at the apartment the next night, Joneser spread out the map of Aspen ski area on the table. A black magic-marker line started at the base, went up the center and then cut to the right. From there it ran up the right side following a string of blue runs before terminating at a point with the word Sundeck. Joneser explained, "We come up through the X Games venue, get through a rope here." He pointed with his finger. "Come across on this service road, through another rope, hop onto Ruthies and basically follow that straight to the top. If it gets too hairy we bail off the side boundary and boondock through the woods."

Sid followed the route on the map and shrugged, "I don't see any better way to do it. It *would* be great if we weren't being chased by that point." He turned now to Cliff who was leaning back on the couch taking a long swig of beer, "So, what did you learn Cliffy?"

Cliff let out a loud belch and held his fist to his sternum then answered. "For one thing, no one left all morning with the cash, it all goes into a drop box in the floor and then gets picked up at the end of the day. You will need a set of cable cutters to open the drop box. I also found where to launch the sleds from, but there might be some kinks."

"What sort of kinks?" Sid asked.

Cliffy said, "Leaving the sleds at the base is a bad idea, I think the sleds need to be launched from a disposable vehicle, something that can be abandoned. The parking behind the hotel is so limited, that anything there for more than ten minutes is going to be towed or at least draw a lot of attention. And if we used Joneser's truck with a trailer, people might see the sleds coming off the trailer, and the truck would never make it out of the valley without getting stopped by police."

He turned to Sid and asked, "Can you get that old school bus running? The one we found behind the welding shop?"

22.

Cliff stood shivering next to the school bus. He had been warm as he walked up to it, but now as he stood there doing nothing, the cold crept through his winter clothes. Sid and Joneser were working to disconnect the two heavy-duty batteries. For tools they had an adjustable wrench and a pair of pliers and neither tool was optimal.

"Cliff!" Sid called in a loud whisper. Cliff crunched through the snow up to the front of the bus.

"What?"

"Try to see if any of the tires are flat, give them a shake or a kick, if it's flat it will have some give to it." Cliff marched off purposefully.

A moment later a loud 'THUNK' resonated from the side of the bus and Joneser loudly whispered, "Fuck." They had gotten the batteries free and underestimated just how heavy they were. Quickly, they picked up the dropped battery and set it in one of the extra-large milk crates they had taken from behind the grocery store. Cliff joined the others and helped carry the batteries over to the plowed road and into the alley as Johnny pulled up in the car. They set the batteries in the trunk and drove away.

The lack of a key for the bus was no longer an issue. Sid opted against hot-wiring the ignition. Instead he had gone to the auto parts store and bought a standard Ford ignition switch that would match the one in the bus. The new switch came with it's own set of keys.

With Cliff's guidance they snuck into the bus yard of his employer. He had looked at the security cameras in the dispatcher's office and knew where the blind spots were. He directed them to two of the spare buses sitting at the dark end of one row. Split into two teams, they opened the battery compartments on each bus. Working quietly, they removed a fully charged battery from each bus and replaced it with a frozen, dead battery. Then they put all the connections back correctly, slid the battery tray into place and returned each panel into the locked position.

They set the heavy batteries in the trunk of the car and Sid added a tool kit, the ignition switch and a small can of gas. It was bitterly cold that night when they quietly parked by the old bus. Johnny and Joneser installed the batteries while Cliff held a flashlight and Sid worked with freezing fingers to install ignition switch. Finally Sid announced they should give it a try. He splashed gasoline into the throat of the carb and worked the throttle, as he told Johnny to try cranking it.

The big motor turned over surprisingly fast for the cold temperature, but when Sid leaned over it to see if the carb was pumping fuel, the engine backfired a ball of flame into his face twisting up the little hairs of his beard and eyebrows. He tried again and the motor roared to life. Dogs started barking blocks away and lights came on in a few of the homes nearby. They let the motor idle quietly and things seemed to settle down. Sid didn't bother putting the air filter assembly on the carb, he just lowered the hood down and fastened the straps. Then Cliff drove the bus out of the snow and onto the plowed road. From there they drove it up to the lower parking lot of the ski area where overnight camping is allowed. The bus pulled right in alongside several RV's and another converted school bus. The guys figured as long as they moved the bus into a different spot every few days it shouldn't draw any attention. They had just commandeered an abandoned bus.

The plan was in motion.

That Sunday they drove the bus to a secluded dirt parking lot where Sid's old employer stored extra construction equipment. Sid started up a portable generator and ran an extension cord to a heavy duty Sawzall. It was noisy work, but they were far enough away from town, that they didn't attract any attention. While Sid ran the saw, Cliff and Joneser used spray paint to black out each of the side windows running the length of the bus. From the outside it looked like incredibly dark window tint. Once the modifications were done, they returned the bus to the ski area parking lot.

Ads for the Aspen X Games started appearing on TV and on the radio. The event would include free concerts at night and extreme sports competitions all day for four days. The promoters were building racetracks and slope style courses on the hill. And the base area would have a fifty-foot tall ice-climbing tower. Athletes were slated in from all over the world.

Early one weekday morning, Cliffy and Sid drove Joneser's truck to the C.B. South trailhead and unloaded both of the sleds. There wasn't another vehicle in the parking lot as they strapped five-gallon plastic gas cans to each running board and headed off slowly down the trail. They had studied the maps and tried to pick a location in the wide valley of Taylor Park for the main fuel cache. When they reached the spot, they took both cans off of Joneser's sled along with two quarts of injection oil and set them in a rocky outcrop behind a stand of pine trees. They shoveled on snow to camouflage the tanks, and Sid nailed a battered NO HUNTING sign to an aspen tree right above the stash to help locate it in a hurry.

Next they rode east and made a cache halfway up Cottonwood Pass. They considered this an emergency plan. If for some reason they could not immediately return to Crested Butte, they would head towards Buena Vista. The logic was that they could hide on the pass and refuel, then double back and appear as if they had come from that direction. Of course, this alibi would eventually fall apart since they had no vehicle parked there, but the team felt a half assed plan B was better than no plan B at all.

With the sleds free of the fuel tanks, they were able to enjoy the ride back towards the C.B. side, but instead of riding straight to the trailhead, they veered off a few miles early and started bushwhacking through the trees. They were scouting a location for one final step of the plan and found it in the form of a small gully hidden between two large rocks. They spread a topographical map across the seat and marked the location on the map. Then they made notes of some landmarks to help lead them back to the gully. Feeling a sense of accomplishment, they headed back to the truck.

A few days later, the guys were sitting in the apartment. Cliff was reading a schedule of X Games events. Joneser was patching a hole in his thrift store jacket. Sid was going through every pocket of their backpacks, making sure there was nothing hidden inside that could be traced back to them. Each of them had a large mountaineering pack that rode comfortably and carried plenty of gear, but was light and sleek to allow for easy maneuvering on skis or a sled.

Johnny was in the kitchen fussing with three pairs of cross-country rental skis from the shop he worked at. He was clipping a boot into the toe binding on one ski and called out, "Are you guys sure you'll know how to use these? Seriously, when was the last time you went cross-country skiing?"

Sid answered, "Uhh, two years ago I took that girl Lindsay cross-country skiing around Peanut Lake. I did ok… with the skiing, not with her."

Then Joneser added, "I haven't done it since high school, but I'm sure I can fake it."

"Yeah I bet you guys will figure it out good enough, hopefully you're not skiing for your lives when it comes down to it." Johnny concluded.

Cliff spoke up, indicating the X Games schedule "If we do the deed at 10:30, women's speed qualifying will be going on at the ice climbing tower, also snowboarder slope style will be finishing, there will be a lot going on."

Sid added, "Hopefully it's so busy, no one notices two sleds sneaking up along the side of the course and hopping onto that road."

23.

Sid and Johnny juggled shifts with coworkers to get the weekend freed up. Cliffy and Joneser decided they would just call in sick. Tuesday of that week, all four of them managed to get free after lunch to get a half-day of skiing together. As they rode up the quad chair, they ran through disaster scenarios and responses.

"What if a badass ticket seller just locks down the booth and won't get out?"

"Full abort, ditch gear and try to get lost in the crowd."

"What if you can't make it out the top of the ski area?"

"Break to the right and get out of the ski area into the Conundrum Valley."

"What if you blow a drive belt?"

"Replace it with a spare."

"What if a sled goes down?"

"Ditch it and ride double."

"What if you can't get the bus into position?"

"Drive up Spring, onto Durant, pick the guys up and then ditch the bus a few blocks away."

On and on it went until they had convinced themselves they actually had a chance at pulling off the most ridiculous scheme in ski area history.

Cliff and Sid found themselves alone for one ride up the hill. They sat in silence as the chair lift cable passed over a set of squeaky sheave wheels. Suddenly the chair dropped a few feet and then rose again as it fell into a bobbing rhythm. Both of them looked up and saw the whole line of chairs had begun to bounce up and down by several feet. The cause was obvious as they could see Joneser and Johnny swinging their skis up and down in synch and laughing. Someone in a chair behind angrily called for them to knock it off, and the bouncing slowly eased.

Cliff turned and said, "You know Rippey isn't your responsibility right? Why do you want to do this?"

Sid thought for a moment, trying to find the right words. He clacked his skis together and watched a handful of snow slip off his skis and drop through the air to the ground below. Sid looked at his friend, and said, "Cliff, even if you hate it, you have a future ahead of you. I really don't have shit. I love skiing and I love mountain biking, but I'm not great at either of them. No one would ever pay me to do it. The reality is, I can operate machinery with average ability and I can sort of fix stuff, but my destiny is a low paying job with my name on my shirt."

"I think you're selling yourself short," Cliff responded, not looking at Sid, but gazing ahead at the line of chairs stretching up the hill. Then he added, "One way or another, this will be something we always remember."

"Or regret," was what came to Sid's mind, but he bit his tongue. He sensed that Cliff heard it anyway.

Cliffy and Joneser each left work early on Friday complaining of stomach pains. They went to the apartment where Sid and Johnny had a big meal of meat loaf and mashed potatoes set out. They ran through the final checklist, loaded bags of gear into the trunk and snapped skis onto the rack of the Galaxy. They pulled up next to the bus in it's secret parking spot and were surprised to find an orange 3"x5" sticker on the door identifying it as an abandoned vehicle that would be impounded on March first. They tore off the sticker and accepted the implication that the bus could now be linked to the town of Crested Butte when it was found later in Aspen.

"So they can trace the bus all the way here. Big deal." Cliff said. "They won't be able to tie it to us." He opened a box of disposable blue latex gloves and slipped one onto each hand, "And I intend to keep it that way."

He and Johnny climbed inside and the bus fired up. Joneser stood behind the bus and led Cliff through a final light check. Sid peeked under the hood one last time to make sure everything was secure. Then, as long shadows crept across the snow and the sun sank behind the mountains, the bus pulled away with the Galaxy behind it.

Cliff felt that the old school bus was a much rougher ride than the nice Thomas Transit buses he drove at work, but he soon had the hang of it and began to appreciate the feel of the big machine. Behind him Johnny meticulously went over every railing, handle and knob with a roll of paper towels and a spray bottle of Windex. He also wore gloves, but paranoia was beginning to overtake him. Every surface of the bus had previously been cleaned and recleaned, but still he wouldn't stop wiping. Cliffy tried to get him to stop, then decided to tell a story instead.

"This reminds me of a true crime story I watched about these guys who pulled a bank robbery." Johnny walked to the front of the bus so he could hear over the drone of the engine and road noise. Cliff pointed to a sign and said, "Please stay behind the white line." Johnny almost stepped back and then realized the absurdity, and smacked Cliff in the back of the head as he sat on the top step leading up from the doorway.

"Anyway, this team of guys comes out from New York to pull a job in LA. They rent a house as their base and they do the job over the Fourth of July weekend. So as the fireworks are going off, they hammer through the roof of the bank and into the vault. They got into the vault and cleaned it out."

"So then what?" Johnny asked.

"Well, they totally pull off the job, and by Monday morning when the bank opens up, these guys are on their way back to New York. Then the FBI gets there and starts to investigate, and they realize that this job reminds them of this crew in New York, but, they have no way to prove it was them. The Feds end up finding the rental house, and they know the robbers used it, but the whole place is spotless. No prints anywhere, everything has been wiped clean except..." Johnny looked up at Cliff, falling prey to the dramatic effect.

"The dishwasher! The dishwasher was full and it had soap in the little thing. It was turned to the right setting but just needed someone to press start. So the cops had fingerprints of all the guys on the dishes and silverware. The cops go and pick them up, with all the evidence they need! Wouldn't that suck? I wonder if they realized it afterward? 'You started the dishes, right?' 'No, you said you would'." Cliff was laughing to himself as he finished the story.

Johnny just looked at him annoyed. "So what does that mean? What dishes do we have to do?"

Cliff turned to Johnny and grinned, "It means you already washed the dishes bro. So just relax and smoke this." He handed Johnny a packed bowl.

It was late at night when the guys pulled into a small town just outside of Aspen. Sid and Joneser found a dark corner of a parking lot at a motel and slept uncomfortably in the Ford. Johnny and Cliff slipped the bus into a row of other buses parked behind the Basalt High School, and rolled out sleeping bags on the cold floor of the bus.

Each of them felt like they had barely closed their eyes when the tinny electronic beep of their watch alarms started going off at six a.m. Johnny and Cliff walked away from the high school in the early morning darkness with their sleeping bags packed. They had just made it into a neighborhood when the Galaxy pulled up alongside them and they hopped in back. They basked in the warmth of the full blast heater and greeted Sid and Joneser. Sid said, "Nice job driving that beast all the way here!"

"Aww, it rode like a dream."

"Yeah, well I don't think I could have done it. You are the man."

Johnny spoke up wearing a look of concern. "So I guess I won't see you guys until this is all over and we are celebrating at home."

Joneser replied defiantly, "Yeah, you and Cliffy get in there and fuck shit up, and we'll come home with the goods."

Sid said calmly, "We can do this you guys. Try to stick to the plan, but if things go sideways just freestyle and think on your feet."

Cliff said, "I think this is a moment when we could put our hands in, and it really wouldn't be too corny."

Joneser smiled and said, "Oh hell yeah!" He and Sid turned to the back seat and all four of them extended a hand and counted to three. Since none of them had much of a team sport background, what followed was a poor attempt at a cheer as they all said something over each other. Someone said, "Let's do it!" another yelled "Boo Yah!" and Joneser screamed an indecipherable war cry. Then they all pulled their hands up and away. Joneser's long gangly arms went too high and he cracked his knuckle on the dome light. Awkwardness aside the cheer did the trick, lifting everyone's spirits while filling them with much needed confidence.

They opened all four doors, Johnny and Cliff hopped in front while the other two grabbed their backpacks out of the trunk and shut the lid. Sid asked Cliffy, "Keys are in the bus?" and Cliff gave a deliberate nod. Cliff flashed a peace sign and shut his door. Sid and Joneser started walking back to the bus as the car slowly pulled away. Johnny and Cliff had a busy morning ahead of them, while the other two just had to kill time and hope no one spotted them or the bus.

Cliffy parked the green sedan several blocks from the ski area. He and Johnny put on their ski gear, pulled skis and poles off the rack, and headed to the ticket booth. They got into line behind a dozen people, and as they waited the line doubled. The signage confirmed that only cash could be accepted, and without any credit card transactions the line moved quickly.

Cliff and Johnny separated as the line branched to the three ticket windows that were open. Cliff reached the window first.

Two young guys and a girl were running the booth. His ticket with tax came to $54.34. He handed the clerk $55 and watched intently as the money went into the drawer on the register. Cliff casually scanned the floor and spotted the round metal door of the drop box. He could see a padlock of some sort looped into a latch. Cliff then studied the clerk- Brandon from Seattle, according to his nametag. He had brown hair cut to a required maximum length, but was rebelling against the corporate policy by having long thin sideburns to his jawline.

A day ticket printed off of the sticker roll and the clerk tore the perforated sticker free and slid it through the semicircular hole in the glass. Then he slid some change and a receipt through the hole and told Cliff to have a good day. Cliff took one last look at the other clerks, and decided they shouldn't pose a problem for Sid and Joneser.

Johnny reached the window being run by the girl whose tag read Logan, Roxbury CT. She greeted him with a friendly smile, but her eyes held an intensity that made him uneasy. Her bobbed haircut reminded Johnny of Amelia Earhart. He purchased his ticket and walked away feeling that she knew everything. Then he realized that was ridiculous paranoia and focused on the several tasks he had to accomplish over the next two hours.

The base area looked vastly different from the last time they had seen it. Banners for the event sponsors hung everywhere and a

135

massive jumbotron was assembled to display all the action and current standings. Next to that stood a fifty-foot tower of ice with a fifteen-foot overhanging wall. A film crew was testing a remote controlled camera that raised and lowered on a cable system mounted to the side of the tower. Loud Alternative music blared from speakers located throughout the venue as the guys walked past several tents giving out free key chains, hats and water bottles. Two new Volkswagen Beetles sat on elevated pedestals. Cliff said to Johnny, "This place looks like the Olympic Village at Woodstock."

"Yeah, no doubt," Johnny said with a smirk.

They entered the line at the crowded main base area and eventually stepped onto the gondola with a few other riders. As the gondola carried them over the perfectly sculpted courses, they scanned the edge of the tree line and determined that even with all the madness on the hill, the path to the access road remained clear- the sleds would be able to reach it easily. When the chair unloaded at the top, Johnny and Cliff bumped fists and gave each other a nod, before skiing off in opposite directions.

24.

Johnny's job was to ensure that the sleds would be able to break through the ropes in a few key locations. Starting at the highest point on the mountain, where the ski area boundary ran next to the Sundeck, he high-stepped through the deep snow over to a bright orange rope that hung between two trees. He tried to act as if he were just taking in the view while he pulled the rope in close and cut through it with a box cutter razor. Then he pulled the ends together and laid one over the other, reached in his pocket and pulled out a roll of black electrical tape and taped the two ends together. The guys had tested several techniques and decided this was the best way to guarantee the rope would easily separate. After cutting the top boundary rope and not arousing any suspicion, he moved down the hill and repeated the process at both ends of the access road.

Cliffy's first stop was at a large map of the ski area that stood ten feet tall. Down the side of the map was a list of names of ski runs and next to each name was a small red light. The lights indicated if a run was currently closed. Cliff saw the red lights on for three double diamond runs branching off of International Ridge. Cliff put his hands through the straps of his poles and skied off in that direction. He reached the top of Perry's Prowl and checked his watch- time was running out. After a quick glance around he grabbed one end of the orange rope that was strung across the ski run and sliced through it with the box cutter. Then he skated to a tree on the other side and started reeling in the rope. Every few feet a short piece of flourescent pink ribbon was tied to the rope, and in the middle of the rope was a plastic sign that read TRAIL CLOSED. He took the sign and the tangle of rope and stuffed it into the snow on the side of the trail. Then he moved to the top of Last Dollar and did the same thing. He had just hidden the rope when a group of snowboarders reached the top of Perry's and hooted with excitement. He heard one yell, "Yes! This has been closed all week!" The boarders all dropped into the run and Cliffy grinned. This was sure to keep the ski patrol busy for a little while. He looked at his watch again and cursed. He needed to get to the bottom fast. He threw the box cutter into the woods and skied as fast as he could to the bottom of the mountain. Cliff was stunned when he saw how the competition venue now looked as crowds started filling in the bottom of the mountain.

The morning clouds lingered in the sky, undecided whether they should stay or go. Crowds of cheering spectators lined the boardercross course. He tried to ski to the bottom, but so many people were walking on the hill in boots and street shoes that he couldn't get through easily. He carried his skis through the last section of crowd and stuck his skis and pole into a rack. Then he hurried into the rental area where he had purchased a locker. Cliff quickly changed out of his ski boots and into shoes. He pulled his gray beanie low on his head, tossed his goggles in the locker and put on his dark glasses. Then he pulled his neck warmer up to his nose and strode out to the street to catch a bus.

Just as he reached the sidewalk, the yellow school bus pulled up and he stepped on. "I just counted four people at the ticket booth." He told Joneser and Sid.

"Thanks Cliff," Sid said. "The sleds are warm and ready. Get into position then disappear. We'll see you in C.B." Sid and Joneser stepped off the bus and Cliff drove it away. Sid and Joneser had hats pulled low and sunglasses on. Sid had his ski parka collar zipped up which covered the lower half of his face while Joneser wore a neck gaiter similar to Cliff's.

They walked quickly toward the ticket booth. By this time, two people were at the windows being helped while a third waited a few steps back. Sid and Joneser ducked behind the booth and opened their backpacks. They dropped their sunglasses into the packs, pulled on the gasmasks and tugged hats back over their heads. They both wore thin mountain biking gloves as they pulled the safety clips from two canisters of bear spray. Sid crept to the corner of the booth and Joneser took up a position at the booth's one door, he carefully tried the knob and found it locked, as expected.

One customer walked away as Sid rounded the corner cutting in front of the next person. The startled man looked at Sid and Sid pointed the can at his face. The man backed away. The clerk in the booth could only see Sid's back and tried to make sense of what was happening. Then Sid turned to face the window and clerk started to say something when Sid squeezed the trigger and unloaded a stream of red dust into the hole in the window. He stepped to the glass and sprayed another shot directly into the booth. He swept the stream side to side and filled the small room with noxious vapor. "What the hell are you doing?" A clerk screamed.

The spray hit the clerks in the booth like a wave of fire. Their eyes began to water and snot poured from their noses as they tried to feel their way the few short steps to the door. The one named Brandon made it out first and started to yell for help. Joneser met him as the door opened and punched him hard in the belly. This knocked the wind out of him and he doubled over and fell down in pure misery as tears poured from his eyes. Joneser turned back to the exit just as a raging ball of fury blasted out of the door with arms outstretched and tackled him by the mid-section.

Joneser fell hard to his back on the brick walkway with his assailant on top of him. The canister fell from his hand and bounced out of his reach. Even though Logan could barely see through her red irritated eyes, she got her left hand around Joneser's throat and with her right fist started driving hard, fast punches into his kidney. Terror filled Joneser's eyes through the glass circles of the mask as he tried to free her hand from his throat with one hand and push her away with the other. Sid rounded the corner and fired at both of them on the ground. The blast hit Logan in the chest and the chemical attack was finally too much for her. She started letting out deep hacking coughs and held her hands to her chest. Joneser pushed her off and she rolled onto her hands and knees vomiting out bile. Sid grabbed the loose canister off the ground and they both dashed into the booth.

The third clerk sat on the floor hugging a sweatshirt to his face and trembling. The robbers ignored him and Sid reached the first register. He remembered his instructions from Johnny: "Don't hit button other than the NO SALE key. It might not say that. It could just be abbreviated." Sid scanned all the buttons and saw #NS on one. He held his breath and pushed it. The drawer slid open. His brain couldn't even acknowledge the denominations on the cash, he was just amazed by the thickness of the stacks under each spring loaded arm in the drawer. He emptied the first register and moved onto the next. He hit the button and it opened to another drawer full of cash. Looking up he could see people gathering outside the windows.

Joneser went for the drop box in the floor and pulled a bolt cutter out of his bag. He was just about to position it when he leaned in to look at the lock again. Muffled through the mask he said, "No fuckin' way." He twisted the padlock free from the latch because it wasn't even locked. He opened the lid and found bundles of bills rubber banded together. Like a bear digging honeycomb out of a log, Joneser used both hands to shovel bundles out of the hole in the floor and crammed them into his backpack. Once it was full, he zipped it closed and –on cue- Sid's watch started beeping. Sid heard it and looked up from the fourth register. "We gotta go!"

Sid could feel the bear spray burning his neck and parts of his face as he rushed out of the ticket booth. He and Joneser skirted between the booth and the large building behind it, side stepping the two clerks sitting on the concrete and wiping at their faces with their shirt sleeves. Joneser and Sid cautiously stepped to the front of the booth and saw a few tourists gaping at them in confusion. The two robbers glanced at each other and broke into a sprint down the sidewalk.

25.

When Sid gave the bus to Cliff, Cliff made the first right turn he could and circled the bus into a loop around the block. He headed down the dead end street to the place he would abandon it. When he first scoped this spot a few months ago the narrow street had been clear, but now three large black RV's belonging to ESPN were parked end to end down the hotel side of the street. Thick black power cables ran from the hotel to each coach. Cliff hoped that his friends didn't trip on the cables as they ran by. The area in front of the hotel's loading docks was still clear, so Cliff swung the bus in and made a three point turn.

Three hotel workers stood on a loading dock smoking cigarettes and watched with mild interest as Cliff completed his turn, backing the bus straight into a snow bank and then pulling forward slightly. A burst of air hissed out as he set the parking brake. He ran to the rear of the bus and released a series of nylon ratchet straps sides. As he released the last one the entire back wall of the bus shifted and dropped at an angle. Cliff walked back to the two snowmobiles and pulled the start handle on the Skidoo. The warm engine roared to life and sat idling patiently. He moved to the Polaris and prayed it would fire just as easily- it did, only much louder. A helmet and goggles hung on the handgrip of each sled.

With both sleds idling in the confined space of a school bus, Cliff walked to the back wall and pushed it outward. The slab of sheet metal fell to the snowbank and slid partially under the rear of the bus. Cliff shoved it a little further as he stepped down onto it while exiting the bus. With the cloud of two-stroke smoke billowing around him, he could have been a rock star taking the stage. Cliff strode through the snow out towards the event venue. With his face concealed and a puffy red parka on. The hotel workers just watched silently, clearly not wanting any involvement in the spectacle they were witnessing, possibly thinking this was a planned X Games exhibition. Cliff waved to them before he rounded the corner. One held up a hand with a half smoked cigarette in return.

The loading docks were typically a peaceful place to grab a smoke, but the next thing the laborers witnessed were two guys in gas masks and backpacks running down the street and climbing into the front door of the bus. A few seconds behind them came two other men who ran to the door and found it locked. One banged his hand hard on the glass and yelled to open up. Bluish gray smoke was curling out of the rear of the torn open bus, but nothing could be seen through the blacked out windows. Then the nasty roar of a three-cylinder motor echoed out of the bus and a sled with a shiny black hood shot out- its rider crouched as he cleared the low ceiling. The sled spun its track for a moment on the snow bank, then found traction and launched over the top. Seconds later another shiny black sled burst out. The rider bounced hard as the skis slammed into the snowbank after a short drop. The driver grabbed the throttle and took off after the other sled.

The men at the front of the bus ran around the side to see the sleds pull away. As they stood there dumbfounded, they turned and noticed the three smokers also staring in disbelief. A huge smile broke across the face of a laundry room employee. He started to slowly clap and said, "Holy shit! That was fuckin' awesome!"

Cliff had rounded the corner and worked his way deeper into the crowd of spectators and tourists milling around the bottom of the mountain where the X Games venue blurred into the main base area pavilion. He casually took off the cheap red parka and stuffed it under a bench. Pretending to be caught up in the action on the jumbotron, he wandered away from the coat without anyone noticing he had left it. Then he made his way across the crowd, dropping the grey beanie in a trashcan and climbing onto the elevated deck of Shlomo's Grill. Suddenly he heard the sound of two sleds cruising through the thinnest part of the crowd. The bright orange pennants waving above each sled looked almost official, and with music and race commentary blasting from the speakers, the rumble of the sleds was somewhat masked.

From his vantage point on the deck he watched the sleds pass under the gondola and move steadily through the venue passing sponsor tents, pedestrians and skiers. The sleds moved safely but aggressively. They were menacing enough that people made sure to get out of the way, but not so fast that they caused the crowd to panic. Once they were through the crowd, they picked up the pace and skirted along the side of the slopestyle course heading for their exit at the access road. They were almost out of sight when Cliff noticed a ski patroller start up a sled and head around the staging area for the slopestyle. He was out of sight for a moment, and then reappeared on the same side of the course as Sid and Joneser.

Cliff held his breath as he watched the two sleds snap the rope and turn onto the road through the trees. A few seconds passed and the patroller turned onto the road behind them. Cliff knew that whatever happened now was out of his hands.

Joneser pointed his sled at the road and the orange rope slipped up over his hood and pulled taunt on his windshield, he nudged the throttle and the rope came apart and dropped away. Joneser saw a long straight cat road ahead of him and mashed the throttle with his thumb. His sled let out a roar and raced to sixty mph. He looked back to verify his partner was behind him, and that's when he noticed a third sled had pulled onto the road.

Sid saw Joneser waving and pointing back and his stomach fell. He had hoped they would make it farther, but he looked anyway and saw a ski patroller in an unmistakable red ski jacket talking into the two way radio in his chest harness as he tried to keep pace on one of the ski area's work sleds. "Well, I guess it's on now," Sid thought as he gunned his sled up closer to the lead. Joneser barely let up as his sled sliced through the second rope and out onto a run filled with people. Skiers and boarders fell down or frantically swerved to avoid the two sleds as they crossed the hill diagonally and made for the opposite side. Once they reached the edge of Ruthie's Run they were on the boundary of the ski area, and they were also directly under a chair lift.

Skiers on the chair lift watched in amazement and horror as the two black sleds screamed up the side of the run with terrifying speed. Sid hung in tight behind Joneser and realized with perfect clarity that his friend actually was psychotic. He and the others had joked about it before, but having witnessed how easily he punched the clerk during the robbery or how he was driving now, left no doubt in Sid's mind that Joneser did not value the life of most humans. Then Sid thought, 'Ok so he's a psychopath, but I'm following him... so what does that make me?'

Glancing over his shoulder, Sid didn't see the patroller on the sled anywhere. When he looked ahead again Joneser's sled had slowed, and Sid pulled alongside him. Ahead of them was the chair lift's upper terminal and two patrollers sat on sleds prepared to block their escape. The chair had been stopped, and two lift ops stood next to the patrollers ready to help with the roadblock, one grasped a plastic snow shovel as if it were a battle-axe. Riders dangling in the last ten chairs watched intensely to see how the conflict would unfold.

The skis on Joneser's sled lifted slightly into the air as he pinned the throttle and aimed dead at the lifty with the shovel. He stood behind the patroller who had angled his sled perpendicular to the path, but since the patroller's sled had no reverse, he wouldn't be able to close the gap. The overworked, underpaid lifty bravely raised the shovel like a batter as Joneser bore down on him. Joneser crouched low on the sled and dropped his head down, prepared to use the top of his moto helmet as a battering ram.

With the terrifying machine racing towards him, the lift op rethought just how much he was willing to lay on the line for his employer. He threw the shovel, which bounced harmlessly off Joneser's hood. The lift op dove behind the patroller's sled and Joneser shot through the gap.

Sid had tried to swing to the far side, but once he was past the choke point the second patroller was quick to pull up next to him on his left. Before Sid could hit the throttle, the patroller had nosed the company sled into Sid's and was trying to push him right off the trail into the woods. Sid's face was hidden behind his helmet, goggles and a face warmer, but the patroller only wore a beanie and sunglasses. Sid could see a furious sneer across the older man's deeply tanned face as he leaned his shoulder into Sid's and the trees grew closer.

Looking down Sid saw salvation in the form of a small red button on the patroller's right hand grip. The patroller was working his throttle with his thumb as the smaller sled pushed against Sid's, and that's when Sid let go with his left hand and slapped the engine kill switch down on the patrollers grip. Immediately the patroller's engine lost power and he pumped the throttle lever in confusion. Too late he realized he needed to pull the kill button back up but by then the engine was burbling to a stop, and Sid was slipping past him. Desperately the patroller reached out and caught Sid's backpack with an iron grip, Sid wrapped his fingers tightly around his handgrips and tore himself free from the patroller.

Joneser had let up to make sure Sid was clear, and as soon as he was, they resumed the mad dash up the ski run. They had only gone a quarter mile when they realized skiers were no longer coming down the run. Joneser slowed and Sid pulled next to him. Joneser motioned off the trail with his thumb and Sid nodded. The absence of skier traffic made them think that the ski patrol had gotten organized faster than they expected. Apparently Cliffy's trick of opening closed runs wasn't enough to fully disrupt the highly trained patrollers. They had used their radios to organize the first roadblock way too fast and the next one might be too much to get through.

Joneser nosed his sled under the orange boundary rope and lifted it high enough for Sid to get under. Then Sid took the lead and they began to boondock though the trees and hopefully to the sled trails leading away from the mountain. The snow was deep and loose as Sid picked his way through the thick stand of evergreens. Joneser backed off and left room in case Sid led them into a dead end. If the sleds got stuck now it would spell disaster. Eventually the patrollers would find where they had ducked the rope.

Sid's sled was lighter, narrower and more nimble than Joneser's so if the trees started boxing him in, the Skidoo might have a better chance of getting out than Joneser's Polaris. Still, every decision was a roll of the dice as Sid struggled to see more than a few moves ahead, and the snow was so deep, he could never fully slow down to gauge his surroundings for fear of getting stuck. He gassed his sled between two deep tree wells, and all the packed snow behind him fell away leaving only loose sugary snow. He made it across then yelled and pointed frantically for Joneser to cut sharply and go around this section.

Eventually they made it through the tight trees and Sid came out above an open V shaped gully leading straight down, it looked like a text book example of a slide path, but it wasn't all that big. Sid calculated the risk, and dropped into the top of the gully. He tried to stay high on one side, but gravity got the better of him and the sled settled into the fall line. All at once the snow on both sides of the gully began to move and slide along with him. He tensed for a moment then realized it wasn't the full snow pack that was sliding, only the most recent six or eight inches that sat on top of a denser, more stable base.

It was unsettling to ride the sluff slide to the bottom of the gully, but he reached the bottom safely and Joneser quickly followed. In another hundred feet they saw the groomed trail they were looking for and decided it might be time to pull the disguises off their sleds. They cut the zip ties holding the flags on and stuffed them into the snow. Coming through the trees had shredded the black plastic garbage bags covering their hoods so Sid peeled the remaining pieces off, revealing the blue plastic with yellow lettering. Joneser's hood was black, but the garbage bag had covered flashy purple accents and the obvious XLT logo. With the sleds back to normal, Sid turned his back to Joneser and asked, "Everything zipped on my pack?" Joneser checked and verified the ends of the zipper were both pulled tightly to one lower edge, then Sid did the same for him. They checked their fuel levels, and eased their sleds up to the edge of the trees to peer out.

The road was clear looking back towards the ski area, however the guys were distressed to see that a dusting of snow had fallen last night and no sleds had been down the trail yet today. Their tracks would be highly visible, but it reassured them to know no one was ahead of them.

"Let's get the fuck out of here!" Joneser declared and launched his sled out of the woods and onto the firm packed trail. Sid followed and they both took off down the trail as fast as possible.

The trail had recently been groomed and was as smooth as a racetrack, so the guys rode it like one. Both riders crouched low and set their feet firmly in the stirrups. Sid squeezed the throttle until the thumb lever was against his grip and left it there. He took a quick glance at his gauges and saw the speedometer steady at eighty mph while the tachometer needle settled over the 8,000 rpm mark. The sleds sped into a long corner and Sid's mind drifted into a quick replay of what they had just done less than thirty minutes ago. He shrugged his shoulders and felt the weight in his pack settle against his back. He had no idea how much cash he was carrying, but he could definitely recall several handfuls of $100 bills.

They left the groomed trail and began climbing up to the high alpine ridgeline. They reached an exposed face at the top of a bowl and could look back down to the tree line about a mile and a half below them. There, coming out of the trees were three sleds. They could be ski patrollers, police, or simply some other sledders out for a ride, having no idea what had taken place. Either way, Sid and Joneser were not slowing down, and as they climbed higher, snow started to fall and the trail turned to flat light. Sid repositioned his goggles and pulled his facemask snug over his cheeks. It was time to head for the high country.

26.

Dan Rickenbacker sat in a comfortable leather chair in the den of his log home, just north of Gunnison. Spread out on his desk in front of him was his gun cleaning kit and his fully disassembled hunting rifle. He was meticulously cleaning and inspecting each piece when he heard the phone ring. He checked the clock on the wall next to a mounted elk head and saw that it was ten minutes to noon. His wife Cheryl answered the phone and then yelled that it was for him.

He put down the piece he was holding and walked to the kitchen. Cheryl held out the phone and said, "It's the sheriff." Dan thanked his wife and then put the phone to his ear. During the short conversation he cocked an eyebrow at the news and scratched an itch in his dark Fu Manchu mustache. When he hung up the phone, Cheryl asked in exasperation, "They want you to go out? Dan, we made plans to have Shane and Emily over tonight."

The big man gave an apologetic look and took his wife's hand: "Honey this isn't a normal call out for a lost hiker. This morning two yahoos pulled a robbery in Aspen, and they escaped on sleds. People think they are either headed here or to Buena Vista. So me and the boys are going to be ready to meet them if they get here."

"What?" she asked. "That's crazy! So you're joining a posse on a manhunt?" She waited for him to say he was joking and he solemnly nodded his head. "Well, you guys need to be careful, are the police going with you?"

"Two of the forest service cops are coming, but they only have the two sleds, so me, Shane and Marvin are just going to assist them," he said. No longer able to contain his excitement, a grin broke through his mustache.

Cheryl let out a sigh and waved her hand towards the door. "Go! Grab your stuff and get the trailer hooked up, I'll put together some sandwiches for you guys."

Dan was well known in the valley as a big time snowmobile rider. He and his friends often claimed the honor of being the first ones to break open the popular trails each season, and he helped out on the same search and rescue team that Rippey had been involved with. An avid hunter and horse rider, with the build of a hockey player he was not a man to be messed with.

Thirty minutes after the phone call, Dan was pulling into the trailhead parking lot in C.B South with an enclosed four-sled trailer behind his crew cab Chevy 4x4. He and his friends were laughing as they stepped out and joined the two forest service police in their dark green uniform coats. They spread out a map on the hood of the officer's SUV and discussed a plan as one of the men drove the sleds out the front of the trailer.

There were three other trucks with trailers parked in the lot, but they could tell by the recent tracks, and the lack of snow on them, that they had only been parked there since the morning. It was possible that one of these vehicles had been left for the thieves to use when they returned, and the police planned to stake out the trailhead and check all the returning riders. Dan was putting on his helmet and straddling his powerful RMK 800, when a Ford Explorer marked with the Town of Crested Butte Police Department shield pulled in with officers prepared to watch the parking lot.

The two tree cops donned brown helmets with bubble visors and rode stock Skidoo trail sleds, while the Gunnison crew all wore moto helmets and rode audacious mountain sleds with engines modified for max power with suspensions and tracks set to climb the highest hills through the deepest pow. The slednecks blasted off down the trail throwing roosts out behind them. As the noise died down, the police headed down the trail at a slow safe pace of thirty-five mph, both of them sitting bolt upright and looking straight ahead.

27.

The weather on the ridgetop trail had come hard and fast. Snow fell like icy pellets driven by the gusting wind. Any trace of the trail ahead of them had been scoured away by the blowing wind and drifting snow. Luckily, they could still clearly see the wooden posts that marked the way. The two friends played leapfrog along the way- one would break trail for a while, and then they would swap positions. The idea was to keep fuel consumption equal since breaking trail burned much more than following someone. No matter how they tried to conserve fuel, both of them were below half a tank, and the big XLT seemed to be burning it faster than Sid's. At this rate neither of them would make it to C.B. on the fuel in the tank. Finding the fuel cache was imperative.

Sid breathed a sigh of relief when he recognized they were at one of the last hill climbs along the ridge. He wondered how close the pursuers were behind them, and whether there might be more closing in from ahead. Sid and Joneser had the sense of being in a vise tightening around them by the minute, and that their best chance was to make it to Taylor Park. Not only would the sleds need fuel and oil, but the guys were getting dehydrated and running out of energy.

Adrenaline had fueled the morning, but as they entered the second hour of hard riding, their muscles weakened.

The last section of the ridge was possibly the worst. Drifts of snow three and four feet high had blown across the trail one after another, and riding through them was like riding a jet ski through big ocean swells. Powering through the drifts also sent waves of snow over the hood and up onto the riders. They were constantly wiping snow from their goggles to regain visibility. On top of that, the snow would plug the cooling vents in the hood. While they rode they kept leaning forward over the handle bars to shovel handfuls of snow away from the vents, trying to provide cooling air to the smoking hot belt and clutches.

Gradually they came down out of the storm. The snow continued falling, but the wind had eased up significantly. Stunted and gnarled evergreens poked out of the snow, but as they followed the trail below the timberline, the trees swelled in numbers and size. Coming down out of the high country lifted some of the dread that was burdening the pair, but it was nothing like the feeling of relief the guys felt when they crossed the first track from another rider. For a mid-season Saturday with decent weather, there would be plenty of other riders out in the giant playground of Taylor Park. Sid and Joneser were counting on this, and they hoped to simply blend in with the other riders and casually slip through the net of pursuers.

They rode past a powder field with several riders out laying tracks through the deep snow. Off to the left two sleds sat empty while their riders helped dig a third out of the massive hole he had put himself into. With each new rider they spotted, the bandits felt a new level of confidence and safety settling over them like a cloak of invisibility.

With a wave Joneser led Sid off the trail and behind a thin stand of bare aspen trees. They pulled the sleds side by side and shut off the engines. The sound of the motor had been keeping Sid energized all day, and without it he slumped back with the weight of the pack. He pulled off his helmet and reached his arms out above his head and twisted his wrists back and forth. Joneser turned towards him and sat with his elbows on his knees.

"Dude, we're doing it." He reached his gloved fist out to Sid who bumped it with his own. Each of them took a water bottle and drank deeply. Joneser pulled two PowerBars from a chest pocket in his coat and handed one to Sid. They gnawed on the chewy bars hungrily. Joneser unslung his pack, opened the top and let out a low whistle as he peered inside.

"How's it look?" Sid asked.

Joneser reached a hand into the pack and swirled it around. "Lots of tens, and twenties all rubber banded into bundles."

"I guess that makes sense," Sid theorized. "The registers overflow with small bills before big ones." Sid pulled his backpack around and double-checked that the zippers were both tightly snugged to the bottom.

"What bundles do you have?" Joneser asked.

Sid held up his pack and gave it a light shake, "No bundles, everything is loose in here. I was just pulling the stacks out of the slots in the drawers and throwing them in."

Sid froze as two other sleds came in close to their spot and then raced by. The noise eventually droned off into the distance, the sound replaced by the rapid beating of their own hearts in their ears. It was enough to spook them both- it was time to keep moving. "You'll be able to find that gas?" Joneser asked.

"I'd better be able to," Sid answered with a nervous laugh, then he stood on his running boards and rocked the sled back and forth. A quarter tank of gas could be heard sloshing in the sled's plastic tank. "If not, we're doomed."

28.

Several SAAB patrol cars from the Aspen City Police arrived at the base area about the time the two sleds were leaving the ski area boundary. They quickly established that the school bus had been involved in the crime and cordoned it off. With them, an ambulance arrived and EMT's were helping the victims who had been affected by the bear spray. The three clerks who had been sprayed directly suffered irritation to their eyes and lungs but had no permanent injuries.

The events of the X Games stayed on schedule, as exaggerated stories about the robbery quickly spread through the base area. The two tourists from Wisconsin who chased the robbers to the bus were interviewed by the police, as were the three employees of the Little Nell Hotel who had witnessed the bus arrive, and seen the mysterious accomplice who had abandoned it.

Despite being interviewed separately, each employee gave an identical description of the mystery man: white male, average build, average height, sunglasses, red coat and grey beanie. One police officer listened to the description come over his radio as he looked out at the estimated 25,000 spectators roaming the base area. He was reminded of the time he worked a Grateful Dead show and was told to watch for a white male, long hair and beard, wearing a tie-dye shirt.

Dressed in his blue beanie and a nice green fleece, Cliff checked his watch: he still had another thirty minutes to kill before he and Johnny were supposed to meet up. Despite his better judgement, he decided he would pass by the bus and just take one last look at it.

He wanted to know if they had missed some valuable piece of incriminating evidence. After casually strolling around the front of the hotel, he turned and walked alongside the enormous black coaches that ESPN used as mobile communication centers. He could hear the steady hum of a small diesel generator mounted in one of the compartments of the coach as he ducked between two of the behemoth machines.

He peeked his head out and looked down the street. Two of the SAABs were parked next to the bus with their light bars flashing. Through the windshield, Cliff could see the silhouettes of several men inside the bus and occasional camera flashes. Cliff noticed orange traffic cones forming a perimeter around the bus and was suddenly annoyed that the bus didn't have the yellow tape that he was expecting. 'Why didn't the bus have CRIME SCENE or POLICE LINE DO NOT CROSS tape?' he asked himself. 'Were they saving it for something more important?'

Cliff leaned back between the two coaches. He turned to leave and found himself being watched by a police officer standing five feet away. The drone of the generator had masked his approaching footsteps. The officer was tall, and his thick winter coat only amplified his muscular frame. "Want to tell me what you're doing back here?" Cliff was speechless as another policeman walked down the side of the bus and stepped behind him.

29.

The two sleds danced through the snow as Sid and Joneser skirted in and out of the trees along the far West side of the valley. If anyone happened to notice them, the guys wanted to look like weekend sledders out having fun instead of violent felons with back packs full of cash, hell bent on a run for freedom. Finally Sid found the stand of trees he was looking for and they pulled the sleds in by the rock pile and killed the engines. "You grab the fuel, I'll get the hoods open." Joneser said.

"Yeah, let's do this NASCAR style." Sid suggested.

He sunk to his knees in snow as he stepped off the sled and post holed to the hiding spot under the old NO HUNTING sign. At least another eighteen inches had fallen since he and Cliff had made the cache and he dug his hands in deep feeling for the plastic bottles.

Joneser opened both hoods and spun the caps off of the gas tanks and oil bottles. The snow was falling again, but Joneser could plainly see about a quarter mile away where a group of four riders were high marking up the face of a steep hill. The sounds of their engines peaked as they topped the climb, then dropped away as they coasted back down the hill. Sid sighed with relief as his hand hit a plastic jug in the snow and he hoisted out the gas cans, then he reached around some more and found the two quarts of injection oil. He screwed the tops off and set a bottle upside down in each sled's oil reservoir. The cold oil slowly glugged out as each of them emptied the fuel into their tanks.

They had stuffed the empty jugs back into the snow and tightened down their caps and hoods when a roar echoed through the valley. Both of them looked up to see two big mountain sleds pass by them and beeline for the riders at the hill climb. They watched as the two riders waved over the hill climbers and all of them gathered in a group. "Oh, I don't like that," Sid said with fear creeping into his voice.

"You think they're looking for us?" Joneser asked.

Sid didn't answer. He just kept watching the other group through the trees and falling snow. He heard engines fire up again, and he got on his sled and wrapped his fingers around the handle of the pull cord. Joneser did the same. But the two loud sleds pulled away from the other group and headed further up the valley. They listened until he couldn't hear the pursuers any longer, and the other sleds started playing on the hill again.

"So what do you want to do from here out?" Joneser asked. "There's probably more of them still coming. I bet those guys were just the quickest."

"We can stay in these trees and boondock for another mile, but then we'll be at the top of the reservoir. That will be the choke point. The only way is that one trail down the side, and it'll be all whooped out." Sid answered, sounding dejected.

"That's not the only way." Joneser said. "There's something I think we could try." Sid looked at his friend, through the helmet and goggles, Sid couldn't see Joneser's expression, but he knew he was grinning. "It's actually more of a 'Do or Do Not. There is No Try'," Joneser admitted.

Once again, the sleds powered through deep snow as they carved in and out of the trees on the hillside above the valley floor. The trees were spread out enough that they rode side by side, each picking their own lines around obstacles. If they hadn't been running for their lives this would have been a great day of riding sleds.

Sid nervously turned his head and looked back for a moment to make sure they weren't being followed. When he faced forward again he realized he had made a mistake. Evergreen trees stood in front of him forming a wall he hadn't noticed in time. Looking for a path down to the left didn't offer any options, so he threw all his weight uphill and tried to bank a hard turn to the right. The outside ski lifted into the air and the rubber paddles on the track dug into the snow. Sid was just starting to feel the machine lift out of powder when he encountered a small rise. Then he heard the dreaded sound of the track spinning faster as it lost all traction and the rear of the sled dug a deep trench in the snow and dropped into it. Sid killed the engine and immediately got to work belly flopping and rolling around in front of the sled like a kid home from school on a snow day.

Packing down the fluffy powder in front of the sled would give it a much better chance of getting free. Once he had done that he moved to the back of the sled and stomped down on the mudflap so he could grab the rear bumper. He was relieved to hear Joneser's sled returning, and watched him expertly ride towards the stuck sled, forming a trail that Sid could use to get out. When Joneser realized how deep the snow was behind these trees, he knew not to park there or he would suffer the same fate. So he passed by Sid closely, then looped back up the hill and parked in a level spot. Then he shut down his sled, and walked through the snow to help.

Joneser made it to the sled and muttered "dumbass," to Sid as they both firmly grabbed the rear bumper. Sid counted "One, Two, Three," and they both yanked hard, trying to pull the track straight up. The first pull barely gained them two inches, so they repeated the lift again and again. Just as they hoisted the track free of it's snowy grave, Joneser looked up, startled. He held up his palm motioning for quiet, but Sid could already hear the distinct sound of a two-stroke engine approaching from behind them.

The two of them crouched down. Sid's sled wasn't free yet and Joneser's was ten yards away through deep snow. If the other sled was following their tracks, there would be nothing they could do.

Luckily, tracks from other riders were scattered through the trees and might be enough to confuse the pursuer. They listened as the rumbling engine drew close. The rider was slowly picking his way through the trees 100 feet downhill from them. They held their breath as they watched the rider pass by beneath them. He was standing on his running boards and scanning all around. Miraculously the tree branches blocked his view of the stuck sled and he continued on, the sound gradually fading into the distance.

"Oh Shit!" Joneser exclaimed quietly. "That was Dan Rickenbacher. That guy is no joke. He's got a sick sled and he knows how to ride it. We need to avoid him at all costs."

"Ok, you give me a ski pull and I'll be out of here, then you get to yours as fast as you can. If we get split up, we'll just try to meet before the lake." Joneser nodded and positioned himself at the front of Sid's machine and gripped the plastic loop on the top of one ski.

Sid pulled the starter rope, and the ROTAX engine didn't even try to fire. He knew that it never liked starting if it was pointed uphill. Three more times he viciously pulled the cord, then he squeezed the throttle fully open and pulled again. The engine sputtered to life and belched grey smoke, the smoke cleared and the engine roared into its power band as the track grabbed for traction. Joneser gave a mighty yank on the ski and the machine rose out of its hole. Sid got it up on plane and brought the machine out around the trees. He eased up on the gas and started to turn back towards the trail at the bottom of the hill when he caught motion in his peripheral. Dan's blue RMK was barreling up the mountain straight at him, wanting to draw Dan away from Joneser, he pointed his sled back up the hill and gunned it.

The Skidoo came to life as it ripped through the trees at full throttle, Sid knew the RMK 800 pursuing him had more power and longer paddles on its track, so a straight up drag race would be futile. Sid managed a grin and realized that if he was the one being chased, it meant he got to pick the lines.

Higher and higher he dragged Dan, and both of them knew that going up lead to nowhere. The trees started thinning out as they approached the timberline and that's where Sid decided to cut back downhill. By that point Dan had closed the gap to about fifty feet. The bigger machine had better climbing ability, but Sid hoped that if they were both flying downhill, gravity might level the field.

He cut between two scraggly trees and turned the skis sharply back down the hill. Dan had been expecting it and used the turn to close the gap even further. Sid saw just how much bigger Dan was than him and wondered if he could use the size difference to his advantage. Sid brought the sled down the hill at a suicidal rate, picking his line purely on instinct and luck. He sailed blindly over a ledge and landed inches from a big tree stump sticking out of the snow. He hoped Dan might hit it and looked back in time to see the big man land six inches from it on the other side.

Sid grabbed the throttle again and built up speed as he headed into the trees, managing to keep a solid lead on his pursuer. He realized every time he took a line through narrow trees he gained a little distance, so that was what he aimed for. Another gap opened ahead of him and he punched his sled between the pines. Suddenly he noticed an ominous bulge in the snow directly ahead of him. The skis of the sled straddled a buried rock. It slid along the skid plate under the front of Sid's sled and hit the track with full force. The rear of the sled bucked into the air and Sid's legs went flying like superman, but he held the bars in a death grip and his body slammed back onto the seat with his legs dangling off the back. He grabbed the throttle again, and pulled himself back into riding position with his feet in the stirrups. Something had to give. Sid knew that riding at this pace was going to destroy either him, or his sled, and he was dropping elevation fast. They would be back on the trail in a few hundred feet.

A flash of terror struck him as he looked ahead and saw old barbed wire from a long abandoned fence strung between the trees directly ahead. He didn't have time to pick another line, so he crouched as low as he could and ducked his head. The rusty wire etched a line up his hood, over his low profile windshield and struck his helmet. Somehow the wire missed the hole in the helmet where his face was, instead it caught right above it and tore his visor off the helmet. Without considering how close he had come to being decapitated, Sid accelerated towards the trail. He took a quick glance over his shoulder and saw a small pine tree suddenly thrash violently as all the snow fell from its branches. Dan did not emerge from the tree line.

The Skidoo glided out of the deep snow in the trees, onto the well-traveled snowmobile trail and took off like a rocket. Coming around a corner Sid saw motion in the trees. He put his fingers to the brake lever, but didn't squeeze it. Joneser had been waiting for him and the XLT burst out onto the trail next to him, together they raced towards the banks of the reservoir and the narrow, treacherous trail alongside it.

Sid tried to recall exactly what lay ahead. They would funnel down the valley on this road, to the right of the road the mountainside would climb sharply into a series of cliffs, and on the left side of the road would be the reservoir. The far side of the reservoir was impassable because of several steams running into it. Each of these streams created a six-foot deep crevasse, trapping any sled that came near it. The road had it's own obstacles that came in the shape of countless whoops formed by the heavy sled traffic that went on for a mile or more.

With only a quarter mile before they reached Taylor reservoir, Sid tried to conceive of how they would evade capture through this next stage. If the authorities had set up any kind of roadblock guarding the trail back towards C.B. this would be the place to do it.

30.

Cliff's mind raced. It had been a stupid idea to come look at the school bus. Why hadn't he just viewed it from the snow, like the other onlookers? Now, here he was, near the scene of the crime, caught looking suspicious. He quickly devised a plan. It wasn't perfect, but it would probably clear him of any involvement in the robbery. The officer repeated, "I said, what are you doing down here?"

"I was just trying to see what was going on over there." Cliff answered, his voice shakey. He avoided eye contact, nervously shuffling his feet and shoving his hands into his pockets. The other officer stepped closer and demanded, "How 'bout you show us what you have in your pockets?"

Cliff pleaded, "Seriously, I wasn't doing anything, I was just looking."

The big cop spoke again. "I dunno guy, I'm just not buying it." He held his hand out palm up and curled his fingers in and out, "Let's see some I.D, and whatever else you have in your pockets." Cliff pulled his hands from his pockets and pulled his wallet from his back pocket. He handed his Colorado driver's license to the man. "Now pockets," the cop announced. Cliff reached both hands into his coat pockets again and then held out his closed fists to the police officers. He rolled his hands palm up and unclenched his fingers. One hand held a blue Bic lighter and a small glass bowl, while the other hand held a clear sandwich bag with a small amount of green bud.

The cop took the items and handed Cliff back his I.D., saying, "Mr. Rickman I'm going to ask you to take a walk with us over to my vehicle."

Johnny had found a comfortable spot in a wooden lounge chair at the Sundeck. From his vantage point he could see the upper patrol shack as well as the section of rope that he had sabotaged in preparation for the snowmobile's escape. He never heard or saw the sleds, but he could tell something was happening. First he saw three patrollers move quickly out of the shack. They loaded a rolled up section of orange plastic fencing into a toboggan towed behind a snowmobile. One put on skis and started down the hill while two others started sleds and drove off towards the runs that Cliff had opened.

Shortly afterward two other patrollers skated off the Ajax Express lift and hurried to the top of the Buckhorn run. They both kicked off their skis and stuck the tails into the snow forming two X's at the top of the run. As their radios crackled with chatter, the two patrollers started stopping all ski traffic from going down the blue runs on the right side of the mountain. A crowd began to form as rumors circulated through the groups of skiers and snowboarders. From what Johnny heard, the consensus seemed to be that the run must be closed because of a bad injury. Johnny watched the crowd in front of the Sundeck grow, and tried to picture how the sleds would get past them to the fake rope. It did not look good. And Johnny found himself crossing his fingers and thinking 'Don't come this way, don't come this way.'

Johnny continued to watch as two patrol sleds came roaring up to the boundary line near the top. One patroller held the rope for his partner to duck under, and then he flipped the rope over his own sled. Once he was clear the two sleds disappeared out of the ski area boundary and into the woods. Johnny grinned knowing this meant his friends had ducked out of the boundary from another location. The sight of patrollers leaving the ski area got all the wild speculations in the crowd flowing again. Johnny felt a sense of pride in the chaos he and his friends had caused.

31.

Cresting a hill, Sid and Joneser looked ahead to see exactly what they had expected. Two Forest Service Police sat on their familiar trail sleds blocking the road. Next to them was a rider on a big mountain sled and off to the side sat three other riders. One officer stood next to his sled and motioned with both hands for them to slow down. Joneser took this as his cue to hurtle full throttle towards the man. Sid followed and watched as the XLT closed in on the roadblock, then veered off the road and toward the bank of the reservoir. Sid saw it as the only option and followed his friend across the snowfield that sloped gradually to the water's edge. Most of the reservoir's surface was frozen, but the ice formed an island that was separated from the shore on all sides. When Joneser and Sid left the snowy shoreline, they had almost sixty feet of open water before their skis hit the ice.

Joneser smoothly transitioned off the shore and onto the water going as fast as he could, his sled skimmed across the water and he stood up to keep balanced. Seconds later Sid's machine left the safety of the shore and sailed across the ice-cold water. Both of them kept the sleds pointed straight for the ice and soon the machines scrambled onto the hard white surface. They looked back and saw the forest service sleds fire up and start down the trail following the mountain sled. Immediately their sleds started getting pummeled by the two-foot high mounds of packed snow that carpeted the trail. Sid and Joneser focused their attention on the one and a half mile sheet of ice they were racing across. The ice was mostly covered with old crusty snow that allowed the sleds to accelerate up to eighty mph making their skis chatter along the hard surface.

At this speed, the riders on the trail quickly dropped from sight and fell far behind. The guys passed through one last spot of sunshine, before the clouds thickened and the snow began to fall harder. The far side of the reservoir came into view and they were grateful to see that the ice extended within a safe distance of the shore.

The southernmost edge of the water ended with a concrete dam that had formed the reservoir, so they knew they had to exit before they reached the dam. They started veering to the right and looking for a good place to rejoin the road. A quick nod between the two of them determined they would aim for a spot that only had a thirty-foot gap of open water. Sid reached it first and eased the sled onto the water. The big track churned the icy water and propelled the machine toward to shore. As Sid neared the bank it began to look much steeper than he had first guessed, the sight made him unconsciously let up on the gas and the rear of the sled dipped lower into the water. Now afraid that he would sink into the water Sid goosed the throttle again and his skis lifted as he made contact with the snowbank. The track dug into the muddy shoreline and the sled blasted up through the snow like a porpoise jumping through a wave. As the sled launched into the air, it quickly became much less graceful. Sid had taken the jump off balance and he and the sled both leaned hard to the left as they started falling back to Earth.

The sled came down hard on its side and Sid was thrown forward violently clipping his right knee on the handle bar as he went past. He rolled upright and the pain in his knee started to register at the same moment he noticed two other things. He heard his sled sputter and die, and he heard Joneser coming in hot. Whatever technique Joneser had used to breach the snowbank seemed to be working at first. Sid got a perfect view of the entire bottom side of the Polaris as it scrambled up the bank in a full wheelie, standing on the rear tip of its track. A highly skilled rider probably could have eased the big machine gently down onto the skis, but not Joneser. In a moment of panic his thumb stayed pinned on the accelerator until he lost his grip and fell off the back of the vertical machine. The now riderless Polaris slammed down and coasted to a stop, then sat there idling happily.

Both riders crawled through the snow to the Skidoo. Together they pulled it into a level position. Then, for the second time in thirty minutes, Sid had to restart his flooded engine. While Joneser squeezed the thumb lever, Sid yanked hard on the rope. The engine spun over without firing, making only a weak sound of 'PUH, PUH, puh, puh, puh' as the pistons floated up and down. Neither of them said it, but they knew that with each moment they sat there, the lead they had risked their lives for was getting smaller. The unknown rider on the mountain sled was closing in fast, with the two policemen behind him.

Sid pulled again, and the sled sputtered to life. In seconds he and Joneser were speeding out of the powder and back onto the bumpy, rutted trail. They looked back and still couldn't see the other sled through the falling snow, but they sensed he was getting close.

Battered, bruised and exhausted, Joneser and Sid could barely stand, but they had to keep going. Sid wiped the back of his glove across his goggles and fell in tightly behind Joneser. Together they railed over the tops of the relentless bumps. Standing in a crouch eased the shock of each impact, but it also burned the limited strength in quad muscles and forearms. Both of them tried sitting when it was somewhat smooth and then standing through the rough patches and corners.

The falling snow brought an early darkness to the afternoon, and intermittantly they could catch glimpses of the headlight on the sled chasing them. Each time they spotted it, the light seemed closer. Sid and Joneser were riding on nothing but fear and adrenaline. The parking lot ahead of them would be full of police, and this asshole behind them was steadily catching up. They entered a long straight away full of vicious whoops, and they knew if they didn't haul ass across it they would be exposed and visible to the pursuing rider. If the guy were close enough to see them, they would never be able to pull their last trick. So both of them grabbed full throttle and held on for dear life. Joneser's 700 triple simply had more power and he was able to pull away from Sid. Sid tried to absorb the impacts of the bumps, but his depleted legs kept giving out and the seat would hammer into his tailbone.

They reached the end of the straight. Sid glanced back and saw that miraculously, the other sled hadn't even rounded the corner yet. Sid pounded over another series of bumps and felt something slap his thigh. He reached back to see what it was and immediately felt sick. His backpack had come open- the front of the pack hung like a gaping mouth, and it was completely empty.

Despair started to billow inside him, but Sid pushed it back. He reminded himself that he would still go to jail if he were caught. Joneser slowed a little going into the next corner, and Sid got out in front of him and displayed the open backpack. Joneser just lowered his helmet and shook his head side to side. The blowing money must have been enough to distract the rider chasing them, because they again seemed to have a healthy lead. With a few hand gestures they agreed on a spot to pull the next move. They chose a narrow, tree-lined section of trail that was smooth and fast. Sid slowed and then turned off the trail between two bushes, Joneser followed in his tracks. Moving carefully, they slipped into the forest and away from the trail. Behind some thick trees, they slowed and came to a stop leaving the engines idling.

Knowing that their plan wouldn't work if they were followed, they sat tensely watching and listening to an approaching sled charging down the road. The rider shot into view and for the first time, they noted that it was a red Yamaha mountain sled that had been chasing them. The Yamaha screamed past them at top speed and the sound of its exhaust gradually faded into the distance. Feeling confident about their hiding spot, the bandits shut off their sleds and continued to wait.

Sid pulled his backpack off and examined it as Joneser leaned in to look too. Both zippers were snugged down right where they had left them, but the zipper had split open along its track, the teeth having been forced open. They also saw a deep tear in the cordura fabric. Neither of them spoke. Joneser knew it wasn't Sid's fault the pack had torn open, but Sid still felt he had failed. Sid looked up, ready to say something, but was cut off by the monotonous drone of the two policemen approaching.

Like the other rider, the two officers rode by too fast to notice the tracks leaving the trail, once they were out of sight, Joneser stomped through the snow towards the trail, snapping a branch off a pine tree as he went. He reached the edge of the trail and swept over the marks they had left as they turned off into the trees. The cover up job wasn't perfect, but it would help hide their tracks until the falling snow could erase them forever.

Joneser was walking backwards sweeping the pine bough across his footprints when he jumped at the sound of another rapidly approaching sled. He was barely off the trail and had to hide. He dove into a tree well and curled himself as small as possible, bending a low branch down for cover. He noticed that his arm was trembling and he hoped the movement wasn't transferred to the branch. Joneser kept his head down, looking only at the tree trunk as the angry sound of the sled closed in, and then roared by. Once it was past he quickly made his way back to Sid.

"Nice work dude, that was pure ninja shit." Sid reassured his friend.

"Was that Rickenbacker going by?" Joneser asked.

"The big man himself. He must have really gotten stuck on that fence line," Sid said, grinning.

"That's how you lost him huh? I wondered what the fuck happened to your helmet. So I guess that's what tore the pack open?"

"Must have. I'm sure that ski patroller grabbing onto it didn't help either. That bastard almost pulled me off my sled," Sid explained, trying to rationalize how he had lost the bulk of the money.

Joneser started to laugh as he recalled the start of the chase. "Man, we created some fucking mayhem today." He held up his palm and Sid gave him a high five. "Should we go home?" Joneser asked.

"Hell yeah, I'm sure by now they've met someone else coming from the trailhead. They'll be backtracking before long."

"Do it!" Joneser said and gave the pull cord a rip.

It took some searching, but Sid eventually found the secret location they had chosen to stash the sleds. After jockeying the sleds into position between two enormous boulders, they shut off the engines. Joneser took off his helmet and tilted his head back. Snowflakes melted on his cheeks and got stuck in his eyelashes. Sounds of the hot engines cooling down blended with the sound of falling snow as both of them sat there motionless and exhausted. Sid felt himself dozing off and sat up with a jolt, then he rifled through the seat compartment, pulled out two bottles of water and handed one to Joneser.

"Do you think the others made it out ok?" Sid asked.

"It looked like Cliff was long gone when we got to the bus, so unless he did something stupid, he should be fine. And after Johnny did the ropes he could have vanished like a fart in the wind. Hell, I hope they both met up and skied the rest of the day." Joneser finished the water bottle and rested his head back down on his handlebars and closed his eyes.

Sid took off the damaged backpack and looked at it in disgust. "I can't believe I lost it all."

"Dude you gotta let it go. For one thing, that's probably the only reason we dropped that guy that was following us. He must of freaked when he saw Benjamins blowing all around the trail. Asshole probably stuffed his pockets full. If that hadn't happened he could have just trailed us the whole way, and then we'd be really fucked. That goddamn Yamaha was hauling ass." Joneser sat up on the seat of his sled. "Plus, when you are railing a bumpy trail like that you can't feel shit, so it's not like you could have felt it open up and then stopped and fixed it."

"Yeah, I guess not." Sid said, starting to feel vindicated by his friend. Sid walked to the far side of the rock and dug down into the snow. He fished out two sets of cross-country skis and poles, then two pairs of leather boots double wrapped in garbage bags and a painter's drop cloth. He opened up the garbage bags and held one of the boots. "Oh shit, these things are as hard as rocks."

"Let's set them in by the pipes to warm up," Joneser responded, opening up the hood of his sled. Sid tossed him two boots and he set them carefully in next to the hot metal of the motor and exhaust, then Sid did the same thing. Sid sat back down and they split a granola bar and the last of their water. Joneser looked at their tracks and smiled, "Our tracks are already starting to fill in, and it will be dark soon."

Sid nodded his head and smiled, "I think we did it dude, or at least we are looking good so far."

The leather ski boots had softened somewhat and the guys swapped out of their snowmobiling boots. They stashed boots, helmets and the useless backpack next to the sleds and draped the white canvas drop cloth over everything. They tucked the edges in tight and threw a bunch of branches onto the camouflaged machines. Sid clipped his toes into the three pin bindings of the skis and shuffled in a complete circle around the hidden sleds, "That looks pretty damn good," he observed. "A little snow on top, and those will be nearly invisible."

"Cool," Joneser grunted. Then together they started silently gliding through the trees towards the drainage they planned to follow. The muted colors of sunset glowed dimly in the west as the snow continued to fall.

32.

After the commotion had died down and the ski patrol reopened Buckhorn, Johnny and the rest of the curious spectators began to gather information about what had happened. Johnny smiled when he heard two bandits had robbed the ticket booth and then escaped on snowmobiles. He also heard about a brave ski patroller and some lift ops who almost trapped them at the top of Ruthie's, but the robbers made it past and ducked out of the ski area property. Johnny carefully listened and gathered as much info as he could, and all of it made him happy.

He skied down the mountain and into the X Games venue, kicking off his skis and sticking them into the snow next to several others. He walked into the roaring crowd cheering for the Men's Final Skiercross race. Johnny's hero Brad Holmes powered ahead of the pack and sailed over a massive step down to take the gold medal. The crowd went ballistic and for a moment Johnny got so caught up in the collective excitement he forgot about his rendezvous with Cliffy. Ten minutes later he walked into the rental shop where they had stored their gear. While he slipped out of his ski boots and put his shoes on, he noticed that Cliff's ski boots were in the locker. 'OK' he thought, 'So he's not on the hill.'

Johnny searched the entire base area, avoiding the countless police officers on the scene. He walked to the car and found it empty. He was starting to get worried when he saw Cliff walking towards him with a shit-eating grin. "What happened to you?" Johnny asked.

Cliff pulled a white piece of paper from his pocket and said brazenly, "I got ticketed for possession of less than an a half ounce of marijuana, I'm glad we smoked as much as we did last night, it would have been worse."

Johnny was speechless. His jaw dropped open and he stared at Cliff in disbelief. Cliff shrugged and continued, "So I have a court appearance in four weeks."

Johnny's shock dissipated and he smiled. "Are you done now? Or do you want to graffiti a bus stop before we leave?"

"Don't be a dick. I was gathering information."

"Yeah, so did I- just from standing in a crowd and listening." Johnny was grinning with excitement. "They made it out of the ski area."

"Well, let's go home and see what they got."

33.

On their first attempt, Sid and Joneser peeked out of the woods above C.B. South and realized they were a half-mile farther north than they wanted to be, so they ducked back into the trees and tried a different approach. Now they were looking down the short slope directly at the back of a large, dark house. In the small residential community of C.B South, land was cheaper than in town, and this was reflected in the size of the plots each house sat on. The yards were much larger and the houses were spaced comfortably apart.

Joneser had spotted the large vacant home one-day while cruising through the neighborhood. It had a Realtor's sign in front and had been on the market for months. All the houses in either direction glowed with signs of life and warmth, so they headed for the house that radiated darkness and poor investment choices. Coming to a stop at the back deck, the guys slipped under the wooden structure and found some shelter from the chill wind that had picked up. They removed their skis and poles, and stripped out of their insulated ski pants, exposing street clothes underneath.

They left the gear hidden under the deck and skirted the house, stepping along the mounds of snow that had fallen off the roof and dodging giant icicles. They left a few unavoidable footprints on the path leading from the front door to the plowed driveway, and they walked down the driveway toward the nearest bus stop looking like two locals headed to town for the evening. The backpack really didn't look out of the ordinary and if someone on the bus did notice they were wearing Nordic ski boots, they probably wouldn't think much of it.

As they waited in a small wooden bus stop, they came up with possible reasons to be in C.B. South in case they bumped into someone they knew. They had just settled on a somewhat plausible story when then bus pulled to a stop in front of them. With a hiss of air, the door folded open and they were greeted by Sam, one of Cliff's coworkers, who instantly recognized them.

"Hey guys! Come on in," Sam said as he waved them up the stairs. Sam's warm smile put them at ease as they walked onto the bus and slapped hands with the driver. They sat down across from each other in the first row. Several rows back a tourist couple shared a seat while their teenage children argued in the seat across from them. At the rear of the bus a few more figures sat in the red glow of the overhead lights.

"What's the word Sammy?" Joneser asked. Sam shut the door and maneuvered the bus away from the stop, then looked up into his overhead mirror to converse with Joneser's reflection. "It's so crazy! A police spokesman just said that they believe the suspects headed toward C.B. South and the Cement Creek Trailhead!" Sam swiveled his shaved head from Joneser to Sid in the big mirror and asked jokingly, "You guys didn't see any suspicious looking characters tonight did you?"

Sid responded, "Counting you?"

Sam picked up two more riders and wheeled the bus out onto the road back to town. A song on the radio ended and the local dj read a news update stating that search and rescue teams had been mobilized from trail heads in Aspen, Buena Vista and Crested Butte to help police locate the suspects. The teams would search through the night pending the weather did not worsen. Also a National Guard helicopter would be arriving tomorrow to help with the search.

Sam was beside himself, claiming this was the craziest thing he had heard of his whole time living in C.B. Joneser and Sid mimicked his disbelief. Then Sam said, "First Rippey turns out to be a fugitive who's been living here for decades, now maybe there are other outlaws living in C.B?"

Sid joked, "Hey, this guy goes fishing without a license," pointing to Joneser. "And I never rewind videotapes."

The bus gently bobbed as it cruised along the dark highway heading into town. Joneser dozed off with his head tipped back and his mouth open. Sid watched through the big windshield as snow continued to fall. A few strands of Mardi Gras beads swayed from a knob on the bus' dashboard. Under the beads a small card taped to the dashboard caught his attention. He leaned closer and squinted in the dim light to examine it. It had the font and flowery image of a Hallmark card, but the title read *The Bus Driver's Prayer. Dear Lord, when my time comes, please let me go peacefully in my sleep like my father. Not screaming in terror like his passengers.*

Ten minutes later Sam pulled the bus to a stop in the center of Crested Butte. Joneser snapped awake, then he and Sid thanked the driver and walked off. "Stay safe Sammy!" Sid called out.

"Yeah, watch out for bandits." Joneser added, Sam gave them a salute and shut the door.

"Well, that was weird," Sid quietly mentioned to Joneser as they walked the final two blocks towards their apartment.

"Hey," Sid said a few steps later. "You keep going down Gothic. I'm going to cut over to Teo. Let's just make sure there's no police stakeout on the Whispering Penis."

Joneser replied matter-of-factly, "That is totally irrational and paranoid. I think it's a good idea."

They split up and made a circle of the block, finding nothing out of the ordinary. Finally they were climbing the stairs to the second floor and unlocking their apartment. Both of them were numb. The backpack was hidden in the closet and each of them took a shower. After scrounging some food from the kitchen they crashed in front of the TV. They each took a bong hit and watched the end of a movie before going to bed. Around ten thirty, Sid was startled by the sound of someone coming through the front door. For a moment he assumed it had to be a police raid, but calmed when he heard the distinct sound of Johnny hitting his shin on the coffee table. He smiled knowing that all of them had made it home, and they were officially beginning their lives as fugitives.

Their first day as fugitives felt much like any other. Joneser and Johnny both had cold cereal for breakfast and made it to work by eight. Cliff and Sid had breakfast and hung out for a while before Cliff went in at ten to drive a mid-day shift. Sid would be going in at four to drive the groomer until midnight again, so he had some time to kill. After Cliff left, he walked downtown and got a coffee at the bakery. He sat near the counter and looked at a newspaper while he listened to the chatter of the morning customers.

Talk of the robbery clearly dominated the conversation. Sid grinned when he heard speculation that the sleds were just a decoy, and the money had been handed off to another accomplice at the scene. That didn't sound like a bad idea, Sid thought. Maybe his back wouldn't be so sore from riding that far with a backpack full of cash. Later two guys came in whom Sid recognized as local slednecks. The men lamented how much they wished they had been involved in the pursuit, and Sid had to roll his eyes when he heard one say that he would have caught the bandits.

Sid had heard enough to know that no one in the general public knew anything valid about the robbery. He left the bakery and went up a block to Crispy's snowboard shop called The Air Up There. He walked in and joined the group gathered at the counter. They were a good bunch of guys and Sid was friends with all of them. They were, of course, also talking about the robbery. Sid was surprised when Mike, the bearded one, announced that he had heard hundred dollar bills were strewn along the trail coming into Cement Creek, and he was going out there to try to find some.

"Sid, you should go out there too!" Mike suggested. "Is your sled up at Irwin trailhead? We could load it on my trailer and go look for some green."

Sid was caught a little off guard, "Aaaah, my sled is down, man. I blew the belt last time I was out and haven't picked up a new one yet. Besides, aren't there a ton of cops out there?"

"It's public land. They can't stop us from being out there!" Mike declared.

"You should definitely get out there then," Sid said, draining his last sip of coffee.

Mike, like many others, did go and try to get to the 'Money Trail' as it came to be known. Authorities tried with their limited resources to contain the area, but riders still poured in from other less used access points like Jack's Cabin and Pitkin. With thrill seekers trying to find loose money, and the six inches of snow that fell that night, tracing the escape path of the suspects proved fruitless. In the afternoon an Air National Guard Black Hawk helicopter arrived and began making sweeps of the area using infrared imaging.

The Black Hawk didn't find the suspects hiding in the woods, but when it made a pass over some houses in C.B South, the heat signature of one garage flared brighter than anything else around. Police did a not-quite-legal search of the residence and found twenty pot plants in a garage full of high intensity grow lamps.

In Aspen the analyses of the bus didn't offer any breakthroughs either. Thanks to Johnny's diligence, no fingerprints were recovered. The owner of the welding shop in C.B notified the police that the bus on TV looked like the one that had been parked in the lot behind his shop, and soon that was confirmed. However, no one had seen the bus leave, or noticed anyone working on it. Eventually a witness stated that she had been pumping gas on the corner and had seen the bus drive out of town earlier that week, but it was dark and she couldn't see the driver.

Descriptions of the suspects' sleds were given as a blue Skidoo Summit and a Polaris XLT, black with purple accents. TV and radio news announcers repeated this information as a very important fact of the case. But anyone involved in the snowmobiling community gave a small laugh when they heard this because of just how popular these two models actually were. Several sleds fitting those descriptions were even owned by the search and rescue personnel helping look for those sleds. Blue Summits could be found in many rental fleets as a 'High Performance' rental and the XLT was about as identifiable as a Chevy truck, since the model had lasted almost a decade without any significant changes made to the aesthetics.

Dan Rickenbacker gave an interview describing the suspects as, "experienced mountain riders." Sid and Joneser accepted this as a point of pride. Dan went on to say, "Police should be looking for snowmobilers who tried a robbery, not robbers who tried snowmobiling."

34.

It wasn't until three nights later that the guys were all home together at the same time. Joneser grabbed the ski gear they had left at the empty house, and on the way home he splurged and bought a twelve pack of Fat Tire beer. They locked the front door to the apartment and retreated into the small bedroom. Joneser pulled his backpack out of the closet and slowly shook the bundles of bills out onto the floor in front of them. The guys had never seen this much cash in a pile and started sorting through it. It was a daunting task. They quickly determined that each bundle had a random number of bills in it, so they broke the bundles down and organized the bills into neat piles.

Cliffy lit a joint and passed it around the circle as each of them counted. Soon they found themselves having to count and recount the same piles two or three times. Finally, Johnny worked a calculator while looking at the piles and pressed the = button. He held up the calculator screen and showed it to his friends while he grinned stupidly. It read 28,624. He pressed the division symbol then 4, and held up the screen again which read 7,156. Cliff started moving stacks around until roughly $7,000 sat in a pile in front of each of them.

Sid was the first to speak. He looked down sadly and apologized, "Guys, I'm sorry. I know all the big bills were in my pack, I should have…"

"HEY!" Cliffy yelled at Sid. Sid looked up and Cliff threw a stack of $20's hitting Sid hard in the face. The stack came apart and bills fluttered around the small room. Sid rubbed his cheek. "Dick!" he laughed.

Cliff responded, "Sid, if you hadn't wanted to help Rippey, we never would have done anything, and we wouldn't even have this much."

Joneser added, "And this is a shit ton more money than I've ever had."

Johnny chimed in, "Yeah me too, Sid. And it sounds like losing that money on the trail helped you guys get away. Plus, it's still messing with cops 'cause so many people are out there looking for it."

"Alright, so who knows how much we lost, but this is our haul," Sid said. Then he raised his beer bottle and the others all clinked against it. "Nice work guys. Let's not make this a habit."

"I'd like to make a suggestion," Cliff said, getting the others' attention. "I was able to see the workers from the ticket booth after everything happened, and those poor folks got pretty messed up by the bear spray. Is anyone opposed to anonymously sending a grand to each of them?"

"Oh fuck them!" Joneser scoffed. "They knew the risk when they took the job."

"I know you well enough," Cliff countered, "to know that you're not serious."

"He's just mad that the ticket booth chick kicked his ass," Sid said giggling. Cliff and Johnny both asked for details, so Sid described the event the best he could. To prove it Joneser pulled his T-shirt up, revealing bruises along his side. This triggered uproarious laughter. When Johnny finally got his breath again he said, "You know what? I want to send that girl an extra grand, just for kicking Joneser's ass." Then he pulled together a stack of fifty $20 bills and set it aside.

Joneser gave in and said, "I guess we could toss them some cash. I'm sure their employer isn't giving them any bonus."

Cliff quickly pulled $750 from all four of the individual piles and added it to Johnny's grand. Then Cliff removed $300 from his personal pile and said, "I'm keeping this to pay my ticket for possession of a schedule one narcotic." He then he pushed his remaining cash toward Sid and said, "but the rest of this will just get me in trouble. I'd rather donate it to the Free Rippey fund."

The others looked at him in awe and surprise. Apparently it moved Joneser, so he spoke next. "I need this," he said, reaching into his pile and scooping a big handful out, "to put tires on my truck. I need this," he said taking another handful, "to put shocks on my sled." He then pinched a thinner stack between a thumb and two fingers. "This is for weed, but the rest can go to Rippey." With that he pushed the remainder of his pile toward Sid.

Sid held up his hands to say 'whoa, calm down.' "Guys, you don't have to decide this right now, you each took a huge risk getting this money."

"*Hello?*" Joneser asked rhetorically. "Do you really think that having a bunch of extra cash will help me work through my impulsive tendencies? Like Cliff said, it will just get me in trouble. Anyway Irwin's not the same without Rippey. If this might get him back here I want to help."

With that, all eyes fell to Johnny. He leaned back and took a sip of beer. He took a sweep of the circle and met each of his friends eye to eye. "Look," he began, " You guys know how much I like Rippey, and I want him to be free. But… I'm sick of dragging behind a sled every time we go backcountry. And your sleds, especially Joneser's, are getting hammered."

"Soooo?" Sid smiled. "You want to buy a sled?"

"Yeah," Johnny said hopefully, waiting for the others to approve.

"I think that's a great idea!" Sid said.

"Fuck yeah," answered Joneser. "We're sick of dragging your ass around."

"Plus," Cliff deadpanned, "you could ride a getaway sled next time we do this."

Joneser promptly hit him in the face with a stack of fifties.

The next morning they all agreed to stand by their decisions on the size of the donation to free Rippey. Sid found a cardboard box in the dumpster and was filling it with cash when Johnny asked, "How do you know Ellen will take it? She could just call the cops."

Sid paused for a moment before responding, "I dunno man, she's old school Crested Butte. She's been here since the seventies, and I doubt Rippey is the only shady person she's ever helped out. I trust her. But if she gives the money back, then we at least did our part and tried."

"Yeah, I guess so." Johnny said with a shrug.

Once the money was boxed up, Sid took a black permanent marker and wrote, *For the legal defense fund of John Rippey* across the top. He and Johnny walked into town with the box. While Johnny stood watch, Sid set the box right outside the door of Ellen Green's office. He banged loudly on the door and ran around the corner of the building. Johnny watched as Ellen looked out the window and then opened the door. She read the top of the box and quickly dragged it into her office. Sid rejoined Johnny and they walked back to the apartment.

The days rolled on, but the FBI never came to the apartment asking questions, nor did a SWAT team ever rappel through the windows. One night, Sid did get in trouble at work. He wasn't paying attention and managed to wrap a hundred feet of plastic orange fencing around the tiller of his snowcat.

Cliff borrowed the Galaxy and drove back to Aspen for his court appearance. He was pleased to find out it was only a $100 fine. Two months had passed since the robbery when Cliff and Joneser parked the truck and trailer at the empty Cement Creek trailhead on a Friday morning. It hadn't snowed in weeks and the season was coming to a close. The snow was in a freeze-thaw cycle and felt hard and crusty in the morning. They carried a small backpack with water and snacks as they walked off into the woods. They made good time since the hard snow allowed them to walk unheeded across the surface and after an hour they reached the spot where two large boulders sat next to each other.

They approached cautiously, checking for any signs that the sleds had been discovered. Surprizingly the hiding spot looked just as good in the morning light as it had on the night they stashed them. Even from ten-feet away the white canvas blended perfectly with the late season snow. Yanking and pulling, they managed to get the frozen canvas off of the two sleds, and Joneser swore that everything was just the way they had left it.

Joneser removed the boots from under the hoods, and retrieved the helmets. Then he opened the small compartment in the rear seat of his sled and pulled out the crushed and wrinkled rubber gas mask. He liked the mask, but felt that getting caught with it would be too incriminating. So he took the mask and Sid's respirator, wrapped them in the rigid canvas cloth, and stuffed the items under the edge of the boulder. Then they piled rocks on top and tried to cover the canvas thoroughly. If someone did happen to find the evidence it wouldn't really change anything.

It took a little coercion, but both of the sleds fired up and sat there billowing grey smoke into the morning air. The XLT easily drove out of its hole, but the Skidoo's track was frozen in place and had to be wrestled free. Within an hour the sleds were loaded on the trailer and the guys were driving back into town without any issues. They dropped the sleds in the alley behind the apartments and wrapped them in tarps for the summer.

The next day was closing day on the mountain, and it went off with all the usual shenanigans. The guys pounded out the last turns of the year and met with friends on the hill. After the lifts closed they invited everyone they knew back to the Whispering Penis for an end of the season blowout. The guys played it low key and didn't admit to anyone that they had purchased the two kegs of beer. They also denied that they had rolled the twenty fat joints that circulated through the crowd.

Night fell and the party raged. It had been a weird, wonderful year and the whole town could feel it. With a head full of alcohol, mushrooms and weed, Sid made his way up from the ground floor, greeting Chrissy and Kevin as they parked their townies in a massive pile of bikes leaning against the building and filling the rack. Chrissy gave him a hug as he welcomed her and Kevin and pointed them to the kegs. Then he powered up the first flight of stairs and raised his arms like Rocky. He heard cheering to his right and turned and found Crispy standing with Arliss and Wes. They shared high fives and hugs. Then Crispy leaned in close and slid a baggie of mushrooms into Sid's hand, Sid looked at the baggie, slipped it into his pocket, and his smile went from ear to ear. He gave Crispy another hug and aimed for the last flight of stairs.

With his eyes half open and a wide grin across his face, Sid took a big gulp of keg beer and set one foot in front of the other as he tackled the stairs like a climber on Everest. At the top, a group of cute girls greeted him with smiles, but he was too messed up to try speaking to them, so he simply grinned and shuffled into the crowd. Blurry, smiling faces tried talking to him as he smeared through the sea of people, he felt people patting him on the back and a warm sense of happiness, but he couldn't lose focus- he was looking for his crew.

Sid found them at the far corner of the deck, Johnny, Joneser and Cliff had just separated themselves from the crowd and stood together talking. Each of them had a drink in one hand and a joint in the other, taking tokes as they told stories and laughed. Reaching his friends, Sid's head seemed to clear, and his surroundings came into focus. He joined the circle, and Johnny leaned in close to make sure Sid heard him over the cranked up sounds of Sublime. "Did you hear?" Johnny said loudly, "Rippey goes to trial next month!"

Sid beamed with joy. "No, I didn't know that. That's awesome!" Sid held up his hand with fingers crossed as the others nodded.

Then Cliff blew out a cloud of smoke and said abruptly, "My Dad found out about my ticket. He told me, 'Don't even bother coming home.' He's not going to pay for grad school, and I'm on my own."

Sid's face contorted into a look of grief, but Cliff smiled, "No, it's perfect, it's beautiful. I'm free now!"

Sid rubbed his forehead as he processed the information, then he looked at his friend and saw the deep relief in Cliff's eyes.

"That's great man," Sid finally said.

Sid looked around the circle. Joneser wiped a strand of greasy black hair out of his face and grinned at him. Johnny took a toke from his joint, nodded and smiled. Cliffy looked at the others and smirked.

Sid felt the realization that every choice he had made in his life had led him to this place with these people in this moment. He was exactly where he belonged in the universe. He looked up at the stars and leaned back against the railing.

The last three screws pulled through the dry rotted support post and the railing swung out into space, propelled by Sid's body. Time froze and Sid was completely aware of his change of perspective as his body fell horizontal and floated into nothingness. He saw Joneser lunge for him and Cliff frantically grab Joneser by the collar. Joneser's long arm shot out and his hand reached for Sid. Sid held the red Solo cup in his right hand and calmly raised his left hand out, missing Joneser's by a foot. Joneser's weight was slipping past the point of no return, when Johnny locked fingers around his belt and pulled him back.

Sid watched his friends take care of each other and it brought him peace. A look of serenity settled on his face as he accelerated into gravity's unforgiving grasp.

POW

Tim Reinholt is a heavy equipment mechanic who lives in Longmont, Colorado. This was his first writing attempt and it was a lot of fun. He only writes when he's not skiing or mountain biking with his two girls or restoring an old farmhouse with his wife.

SEASON PASS

1997 ASSOCIATE 1998

TIM REINHOLT   15007946